EMOTIONAL FREEDOM
THROUGH SPIRITUAL WISDOM

Also by Sirshree

* Spiritual Masterpieces- Self Realisation books for serious seekers *

The Secret of Awakening
Secret of the Third Side of the Coin : Unravelling Missing Links in Spirituality
100% Karma : Learn the Art of Conscious Karma that Liberates
100% Wisdom : Wisdom that leads you to experience and be established in your true nature
You are Meditation : Discover Peace and Bliss Within
Essence of Devotion : From Devotee to Divinity
Dip into Oneness : Beyond Knower, Known and Knowing
The Unshaken Mind : Discovering the Purpose, Power and Potential of your mind
The Greatest Freedom : Discover the key to an Awakened Living
Seek Forgiveness & be Free : Liberation from Karmic Bondage
Passwords to a Happy Life : The Art of Being Happy in all Situaltion
The Light of Grace : Why Guru, God, Grace and You are one
Why Jesus Didn't Work A Miracle During Crucifixion
Secrets of Shiva

* Self Help Treasures - Self Development books for success seekers *

The Source of Health: The Key to Perfect Health Discovery
Inner Ninety Hidden Infinity : How to build your book of values
Discover Your Real Wealth : If Money is the Means then What is the End
The Source for Youth : You have the power to change your life
Inner Magic : The Power of self-talk
The Five Supreme Secrets of Life : Unveiling the Ways to Attain Wealth, Love and God
Freedom from Failure : 7 Spiritual Secrets that Transform Failure into a Blessing
You are Not Lazy : A story of shifting from Laziness to Success
Freedom From Fear, Worry, Anger : How to be cool, calm and courageous
Mastering the Art of Decision Making : How to Make the Highest Choice
Complete Parenting : How to raise your child with grace

* New Age Nuggets - Practical books on applied spirituality and self help *

Awaken the Power of Faith : When you can See, then there is no need to Believe
The Source : Power of Happy Thoughts
Secret of Happiness : Instant Happiness - Here and Now!
Excuse me God... : Fulfilling your wishes through the Power of Prayer and Seed of Faith
Help God to Help You : Whatever you do, do it with a smile
Ultimate Purpose of Success: Achieving Success in all five aspects of life
Celebrating Relationships : Bringing Love, Life, Laughter in Your Relations
Everything is a Game of Beliefs : Understanding is the Whole Thing
Emotional Freedom Through Spiritual Wisdom
The Miracle Mind : How to master your mind before it masters you
The Power of Present : Experience the Joy of the Now

* Profound Parables - Fiction books containing profound truths *

Beyond Life : Conversations on Life After Death
The Source @ Work : A Story of Inspiration from Jeeodee
The One Above : What if God was your neighbour?
The Warrior's Mirror : The Path To Peace
Master of Siddhartha: Revealing the Truth of Life and After-life
Put Stress to Rest : Utilizing Stress to Make Progress

EMOTIONAL FREEDOM
THROUGH SPIRITUAL WISDOM

How to take charge of your emotions

Author of the bestseller *The Source*
SIRSHREE

EMOTIONAL FREEDOM THROUGH SPIRITUAL WISDOM

By **Sirshree** Tejparkhi

Copyright © Tejgyan Global Foundation

All Rights Reserved 2017

Tejgyan Global Foundation is a charitable organization with its headquarters in Pune, India

ISBN : 978-81-8415-665-2

Published by WOW Publishings Pvt. Ltd., India

First edition published in August 2017

First reprint in January 2020

Copyrights are reserved with Tejgyan Global Foundation and publishing rights are vested exclusively with WOW Publishings Pvt. Ltd. This book is sold subject to the condition that it shall not by way of trade or otherwise, be lent, resold, hired out, or otherwise circulated without the publisher's prior written consent in any form of binding or cover other than that in which it is published and without a similar condition including this condition being imposed on the subsequent purchaser and without limiting the rights under copyright reserved above, no part of this publication may be reproduced, stored in or introduced into a retrieval system, or transmitted, in any form, or by any means, electronic, mechanical, photocopying, recording or otherwise, without the prior written permission of both the copyright owner and the above-mentioned publisher of this book. Any person who does any unauthorized act in relation to this publication may be liable to criminal prosecution and civil claims for damages.

Although the author and publisher have made every effort to ensure accuracy of content in this book, they hereby disclaim any liability to any party for any loss, damage, or disruption caused by errors or omissions, resulting from negligence, accident, or any other cause. Readers are advised to take full responsibility to exercise discretion in understanding and applying the content of this book.

*This book is dedicated to
Lord Shiva
who neither ingested nor expelled
the poison of negative emotions,
which taught us the secret
of handling emotions with wisdom.*

Contents

Preface	*The Path to Emotional Freedom*	ix

Section I: Q & A
FOR UNDERSTANDING EMOTIONS
& ENHANCING EMOTIONAL MATURITY

Question 1	What is Emotional Intelligence	3
Question 2	Role of EQ in Achieving Success	6
Question 3	18 Locations of Emotions	8
Question 4	Dealing with Emotions of Children	13
Question 5	Long-Term Effects of Painful Childhood Emotions	17
Question 6	Three Ways of Perceiving Events	21
Question 7	Crying is Good	23
Question 8	Knots of Emotions	25

Question 9	Body, Mind, and Feelings	28
Question 10	Responding to Anger	30
Question 11	Anger is a Mask	34
Question 12	Emotionless Communication for Emotional Maturity	37
Question 13	Dealing With Painful Emotions	39
Question 14	Sorrow Related to Events	44
Question 15	Distress on Seeing Others Suffer	47
Question 16	Feeling of Insecurity or Incapability	50
Question 17	Uncomfortable Feelings and Neural Pathways	55
Question 18	Creating New Pathways in the Brain	59
Question 19	Difference Between Emotions and Feelings	63
Question 20	Everlasting Peace and Joy	65

Section II: EIGHT METHODS TO RELEASE NEGATIVE EMOTIONS & ACHIEVE EMOTIONAL FREEDOM

How to Attain Emotional Freedom		75
Method 1	Share With the Right Person	84
Method 2	Consider Emotions As Paying Guests	87
Method 3	Ask Yourself the Right Question	91
Method 4	Use This Powerful Mantra	97
Method 5	Practice Meditation	101
Method 6	Witness Emotions With Detachment	107
Method 7	Do Not Consider Yourself As the Body	111

Method 8	Focus on What You Want	118
How to Use The Eight Methods		123

Section III: A POWERFUL ANALOGY TO SUMMARIZE EMOTIONAL FREEDOM

Your Five-Star Hotel	129
A Hideout of Negative Emotions	
Five-Star Hell	133
Payment of Wisdom, Love, and Confidence	
How to Collect Your Payment	136
Practice Sadhana Consistently	

Preface

THE PATH TO EMOTIONAL FREEDOM

Why's there a storm in the heart and fire in the eyes?

Why's every individual away from one's true self,
which is glorious and wise?

These are some words that express how we feel or what emotions we are going through. *Storm in the heart* and *fire in the eyes* are nothing but metaphors used to describe our painful emotions. Emotions are an integral part of every human being and affect every aspect of our life. It is now accepted that emotional quotient (EQ) is as important as intelligence quotient (IQ), if not more, for a happy and successful life. However, most people don't know how to handle emotions with maturity, that is why their emotions often get out of control. In such situations, people hurt others or themselves and may even fall prey to various addictions. Taking charge of emotions and attaining emotional freedom, is an art, which we all need to learn.

> Ancient Hindu scriptures narrate the epic story of 'Churning of the Ocean.' According to this story, when the ocean was churned during the war between the gods and demons, it yielded the nectar of immortality as well as the deadliest poison that could destroy all creation. Both the gods and the demons were more than ready to partake the nectar, but when it came to the poison, all of them backed away. The horrendous effects of the toxin were spreading throughout the universe, and there was great turmoil and uproar from all directions. Lord Shiva stepped up to consume the lethal poison in order to save the world.
>
> He drank the poison but did not gulp it down and instead retained it in his throat with the help of his inner strength. This is how his own body as well as the rest of creation was saved from annihilation. It is because of this poison that Lord Shiva is depicted in pictures with a blue throat and also referred to as *Neelkanth* (one with a blue throat).

You may have heard this story before, however, let us see what can we learn from it.

We are aware of the fact that, whatever we eat, passes through our throat and reaches our stomach. If we have consumed something wrong, it not only causes trouble in the stomach but also affects the whole body. The same thing happens with our emotions too. When emotions are gulped down, they cause problems. This means when we let emotions enter deep within us, they affect not only the mind but every aspect of our life—be it physical, social, financial, or spiritual.

Lord Shiva knew that expelling or ingesting the poison, both could be disastrous. Similarly, we should be aware that venting indiscriminately or suppressing our emotions, both can be harmful.

Man knows only two ways of dealing with unpleasant emotions. First is to suppress them, which eventually leads to physical and mental ailments. The other method is to express them by shouting, screaming, and blaming others. You may have observed that in situations like these, when a person shouts and screams, he does find some relief. However, he fails to notice what the other individual who was the target of his venting goes through. Sometimes, even positive emotions such as over-excitement can prove to be dangerous. There have been cases of people getting a heart attack on hitting a jackpot and also of people who commit wrong actions in their over-excitement, which causes harm to others.

Since both suppressing and expressing emotions hurtfully can be detrimental, we now need to rise above both these ways. *Shiv sadhana* or practicing spiritual wisdom is the supreme method of handling emotions. We shall learn all about it in this book. This method will help us cultivate inner strength and take charge of our emotions, instead of suffering due to them. We can thus achieve emotional freedom. With this practice, you can not only master your emotions, but also convert them into something beautiful. This can be accomplished only by consistent practice. By doing so, all emotions, even negative ones, can be transformed into a blessing. Is this really possible? Let's understand this with an example.

> There was once a singer who had not yet attained any recognition in his field. He was in love with a girl. When he sent a marriage proposal to the girl's family, her father rejected it outright, saying he won't give his daughter's

hand to some street singer. The girl was soon married off to someone else.

This singer did not gulp down his emotion and neither voiced it out, instead he resolved: "I will be a great singer one day. I will earn name and fame. I will be such a singer that every father would wish to marry his girl to me."

He practiced day and night, and eventually became a renowned singer. One fateful day, the same girl approached him for an autograph. Surprised but happy to see her, he observed, "Whatever happened was for the best; otherwise I wouldn't have become what I am today."

There are many singers today who are loved for the pain in their voice. People can feel their agony in their singing. Such singers too earn name and fame, and for that they thank the harsh times they have faced in their lives.

We need to do the same with our emotions. We must handle them with wisdom and transform the pain arising in us. Consistent practice will help us develop emotional maturity and achieve emotional freedom. The beautiful song that will then emerge from within, will surprise us too.

This doesn't mean that you are being asked to become a singer. But let the songs from your throat and actions from your body flow. Sing such songs (i.e. perform such karma) which touch people's hearts and serve them for their highest welfare. In this way, practice *Shiv Sadhana* and transform your emotions into nectar.

You will come to know how exactly this can be done in the following pages. In Section I, we will discover the answers to various questions on emotions, which will help us gain an in-depth understanding of emotions as well as how to take charge of certain specific emotions in the best manner. In Section II, we will learn how to attain emotional freedom using 8 powerful methods of releasing negative emotions. We will also understand how to transcend emotions to discover our true, divine self. Section III presents a beautiful analogy for visualizing and summarizing the main content of this book.

So, let's begin the journey to emotional freedom through spiritual wisdom. This is what will help you lead a blissful and fulfilling life… filled with nectar.

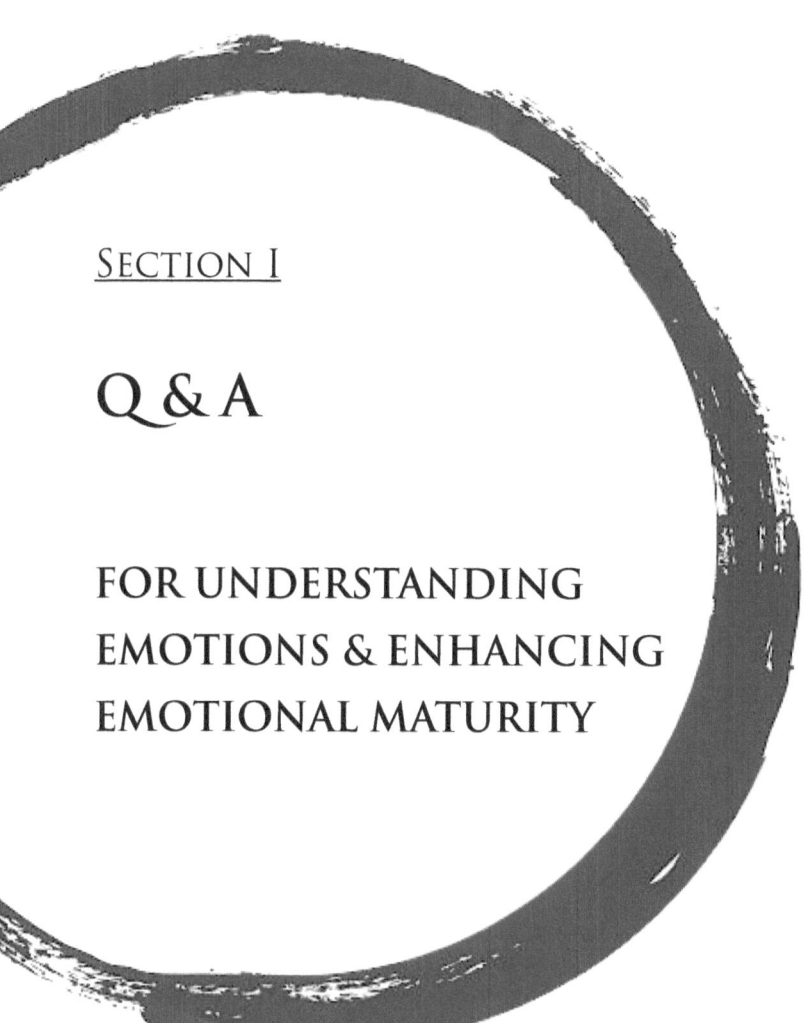

Section I

Q & A

For Understanding Emotions & Enhancing Emotional Maturity

WHAT IS EMOTIONAL INTELLIGENCE

Q. What is emotional intelligence or EQ (emotional quotient)? What is its importance?

> A boy returned home late at night. His mother opened the door and asked him, "Why are you so late?!" He replied, "Mom, I had gone to watch an emotional film. It's called *Dear Mom*."
>
> His mother said, "Alright, come in and now watch *Dreadful Dad*."

From this conversation, it is evident that one is unable to understand the feelings of the other and also mocks them. To understand others' feelings, it is essential to have emotional intelligence.

Suppose one's moods keep changing and one is unable to bear those changes. Or a person cannot tolerate someone pulling their leg, and gets angry or miserable and starts crying. Some individuals simply cannot bear the slightest criticism, rejection, setback, or failure. Some people constantly share their woes with everyone or pour their hearts out to anyone who asks how they're doing. While some derive pleasure from being emotional and weeping. All of these are examples of lack of emotional maturity or low emotional intelligence.

Let us understand what emotional intelligence is. It's emotional intelligence that tells you:

- How to look at the emotions that arise within you
- How to take ownership of your emotions
- How to get your feelings under control
- How to express your emotions
- How to express your emotions when faced with a sudden situation, event, or someone's reaction
- How to understand emotions of others and then how to behave with them

Understanding your own as well as others' emotions is an art. Those who are proficient in this art are the ones who are successful in every aspect of their lives. They prove to be the real leaders. They don't just become successful but also stay successful.

Thus, those who wish to attain success must first resolve to learn the art of emotional intelligence, especially the youth. They must regularly study and practice it. It is a boon to those learning it. It helps to progress both externally and internally.

We often hear people complaining, "No one understands me… no one understands my feelings… no one wants to understand me…" and so on. If you feel that after learning the art of emotional intelligence, people (spouse, sibling, parents, boyfriend/girlfriend, selfish friends, boss, and others) will not only understand you, but also obey you, then you are mistaken. Because it is you who has learnt this art; they haven't. Apart from this, you must also give up depressing thoughts like, "Nothing can happen now… people simply cannot and won't understand me…" The reality is that it is not necessary for everyone to completely understand your feelings. Some will understand you, while some may not.

Everyone wishes to be calm and collected. Everyone loves mental peace but instead of being cool, they create chaos. Why does this happen? They say, "I didn't want to say anything, I didn't want to get angry but I just couldn't stop myself." They never realize when their desire for calm changes to chaos. They may spend their entire life in this chaos. Hence, it is critical to witness, understand, and release your negative emotions in the right manner.

Due to lack of emotional intelligence or emotional maturity, we don't just spoil most things in our lives but also give rise to several problems, and gain only discontent in return. We feel this discontent with everyone—our family, friends, relatives, neighbors, colleagues, and bosses. This dissatisfaction grows like a parasitic vine in the body and mind, clutching and suffocating. We want to flee from this suffocation. But are we able to? Our attempt to escape continues all our life and we are never able to find contentment. Why's that so? Because we can run away from situations and circumstances, but we cannot run away from ourselves.

Realizing our mistakes makes us mature and strong. Realizing and accepting our wrong behaviors is inner strength and emotional maturity. This is what will lead us towards contentment and peace. Thus, emotional intelligence is very important for each one of us.

ROLE OF EQ IN ACHIEVING SUCCESS

Q. What is the role of EQ or Emotional Quotient in achieving success?

People place a lot of importance on IQ or Intelligence Quotient. If you want to be successful in life, indeed you must have a good IQ. However, if you desire true success, it is imperative that good IQ be accompanied by high EQ or Emotional Quotient as well.

Parents get their children's IQ tested and strive to enhance it. But do they do anything for enhancing their children's EQ or even their own?

Whatever the field of work, successful accomplishment of any project or task involves emotions, as they play a vital role. In the field of sports, importance is given to physical and mental training. At the international level of sports, special training is also given for keeping emotions in check and directing them towards the desired goals. This is because it has been observed that those who have a good emotional quotient tend to have a good intelligence quotient too, and are generally more successful. When intelligent people are unable to control their emotions, they fail to make the right decisions and consequently face failure.

Whether an individual is a teacher, a doctor, a scientist, or an artist, emotions play a crucial role in everybody's work. And emotions play their role in the best manner only when they are expressed in the right way. The problem is that most of us are taught to suppress our emotions right from childhood. Males are especially taught: "Men/boys never cry… Men should not overly express their feelings… Men should remain tough… Men should not do household chores…," etc. When children notice women expressing their sorrow by crying, while men remaining tough and stoic, they subconsciously get conditioned in the same way over a period of time.

It's now time to transcend this orthodox conditioning and boost our emotional quotient in order to achieve true success.

18 LOCATIONS OF EMOTIONS

Q. To raise our EQ, how do we begin?

In order to enhance our emotional quotient, we need to gain an in-depth understanding of emotions. Let us begin by finding out where emotions reside within the body.

There are 18 spots in our body where we feel emotions. Each emotion has its own specific spot. Exactly where do we feel emotions like anger, worry, anxiety, joy, remorse, guilt, shame, excitement, lust, fear, hatred, or envy? Training ourselves to identify and locate emotions is an essential step towards emotional mastery.

In this training, you have to start watching where you feel which emotion. This will enable you to understand how to look at these emotions in a way that instead of getting entangled by them, you can release them and free yourself from them, especially from the negative emotions. Otherwise, people often see emotions in such a manner that those emotions go and reside deep within their minds. Those emotions get recorded in a way that they form emotional knots. This leads to physical and mental problems.

Let us now learn about the spots where these emotions are felt. Out of total 18 spots, 5 main spots are in your chest area: east, west, north, south, and center. Some emotions affect the upper side of your chest in a way that you feel like your heart has jumped up. Some emotions are felt in the lower chest area, some on the left, and some on the right. This means on all four sides of the heart. Different emotions can be experienced in these five locations on the chest.

In the same way, the next five spots are around the navel. Above, below, left, right, and in the center of the navel. Two spots are on the two lungs and the other two spots on the two shoulders. This makes it a total of 14 spots. The remaining four spots are on the hands, feet, back, and head. Tingling and numbness in your hands and feet, feeling faint, and so forth, is most often the impact of emotions on your body. Henceforth, when emotions strike, check in which spot do you feel the emotion and how does it feel. This is the art that we need to learn.

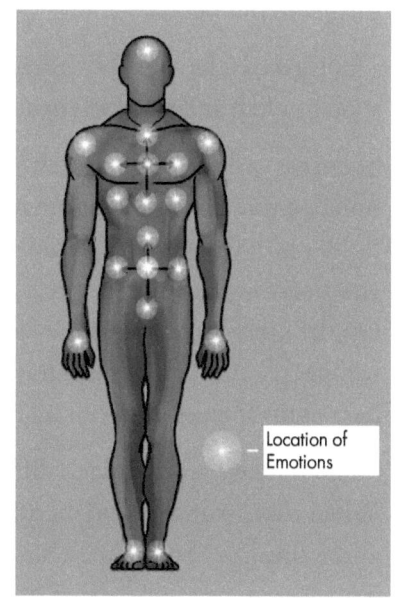
Location of Emotions

The emotion of **fear** is felt just above the navel, in your stomach. That's why, you often feel queasiness in the stomach when you are anxious or fearful. You may also feel heaviness around the chest area. Sometimes the location of this heaviness keeps changing and at times it remains fixed in the same spot. This heaviness is different from that which is felt due to a disease because it is caused by emotions. At times, the effect of the emotion is felt throughout the body. We have to learn to dissolve the emotion and then disperse it. While learning to do so, remember that any emotion will take some time to dissolve. Ensure that you neither resist it nor accumulate it.

Have you noticed that when the emotion is of intense joy or sorrow, tears start flowing? **Eyes are the windows to our heart.** When tears flow, they can be seen by others too. What was inside can now be seen outside. Your breath becomes short and quick, and you feel anxious. When this happens, it means you have been assaulted by emotions. In such situations, breathe deeply and witness your emotions with the right understanding. We will learn about this further in this book.

Often **greed** is felt just above the navel, **love** is felt much above that spot, but **lust** and **excitement** are felt below the navel.

Shame as well as **shyness** are felt in the whole body. A newly married bride's entire body language may express her shyness or a kid may feel bashful while being introduced to new people. Though this emotion may feel uncomfortable but it does not cause suffering. On the other hand, when the feeling is of **shame, guilt,** or "what will people think," it causes misery. This is the fine line that can help us distinguish between shame and shyness.

Sometimes we are unable to differentiate between two emotions. When you can understand the difference, it means you have arrived at the fine line. Sometimes, we misunderstand one emotion for another. For example, what we consider to be love is often longing or attachment. The fine line is between this attachment and love. To know the difference between the two, observe where the emotion is felt in your body.

During the epic war of Mahabharata, whichever emotion Arjuna felt became the basis for each of the 18 chapters of the *Gita*. We come to know about all the emotions through Arjuna in these 18 chapters. We are all like Arjuna. We experience all the emotions—nine positive and nine negative. The chest area where we feel joy, is the same area where we feel hurt too. Isn't this a wonder? When you have mastered the art of seeing such wonders, you will be able to differentiate between the positive and negative emotions. You can then be free of them, without suppressing them or getting overpowered by them. Remaining steady, you will be capable of taking the right decision even in their presence.

Taking the right decision at the right time is the main thing. By swaying with emotions, you are unable to make the right choices or the right decisions. You find it difficult to investigate whether the emotions that are welling up within you are minor or major or deceptively major in nature. Whether they are the truth or false and deceptive. Decisions are right only when they are taken without getting carried away by any emotion. This is known as emotional maturity.

Merely growing up in years is not a sign of emotional maturity. Being able to experience emotions without being affected by them and seeing them in their true form, is what makes you emotionally mature.

Therefore, whatever is happening within you, you have to learn the art of feeling it and watching it, as is. Learn to identify the nine positive and nine negative emotions and the locations where they commonly occur. With the practice of meditation, the understanding of emotions will become simpler.

DEALING WITH EMOTIONS OF CHILDREN

Q. How should we deal with emotions in our children, particularly when they cry angrily or break things?

There is a well-known Hindi song, the lyrics of which translate to:

Don't cry O little one... even if your toy has broken.
Sleep quiet O little one... even if your dream has shattered.

This is what most of us teach our children. The reality is that whenever any feeling is suppressed, it is expressed sooner or later in a violent form. Suppose a kid is crying, and instead of pacifying him by explaining properly to him, he is forced to shut up. He releases this pent up emotion by breaking or damaging his toys. Toys are his own, so he can vent his anger upon them; although many children are not even given this freedom. On growing up, these kids become aggressive and violent in nature; and they vent their anger on the people around them. Alternatively, some of them become timid and always live fearfully. They fail to develop self-confidence.

If parents are wise, they realize that if their kid is breaking objects, it means he is trying to express his anger. If parents are not understanding in nature, they often react by yelling or hitting their kids.

If parents are aware of the importance of emotions, as well as they know how to control emotions and give them the right direction, in that case they can be helpful in improving their children's emotional intelligence. They realize that their child is releasing his emotion if he has taken to crying. They do not consider him wrong; instead they sit with him, hug him, and try to soothe him to convey their support.

A little kid may not be able to express his feeling in words, but if the parents are understanding, they would extract the truth by gently probing him and asking him the right questions. For example, "Are you feeling scared of something? Are you angry at someone? Has someone hurt you?" With the aid of these questions, the child will be able to understand different feelings and identify his own emotions. He will also be able to direct his emotions along the right course.

If a kid comes home after doing something wrong or has a fight with his siblings, then instead of directly reprimanding him, the right thing to do is to find out the reason from him and then guide him accordingly. When a child is trained in this manner, then on growing up he can balance his emotions and is able to attain great success in his career and his life.

Many a time, trying hard to understand their child and solve his problem, the parents unwittingly end up enhancing his problem. When a baby cries in his crib, he is shown a toy and he stops crying for some time. He is engaged with the toy for a while, but then starts crying again. Parents then lift him and carry him in their arms, speaking various things to him. The baby cries aloud even more. Parents are unable to figure out what to do. In fact, all that is required at that time is to take the child in your lap and softly caress him. There is no need to talk to him. Though he needs your support but he also desires some peace. Thus, whether a child is in the crib or in school or college, you must convey that you are available to support him, whatever be the situation. Then give him the peace or the space that he desires.

We always order kids around, but we should also learn to respect them. We should do the same for the kid that resides within us—our inner child.

If even one member of the family is emotionally mature, children can learn the right way to communicate. Else, kids that are raised with aggression and beatings, believe in communicating in the same manner on growing up. They either vent their feelings in destructive ways or suppress them. They do not know how to balance their emotions.

On the other hand, children who are given adequate time and support while growing up, know how to balance their emotions and believe in love. They turn out to be responsible citizens and are capable of creating and becoming part of a highly evolved society.

They remember their childhood days, when even though they whined and wailed and were stubborn, they were always supported by their parents. The love of their parents never diminished for them. Such children believe in love. Whatever the situation, they try to solve it with love. Kids who have had ample support from their parents in childhood, never get troubled by the feeling of insecurity. They simply lose the fear of losing something. That is why, they never get the thought of taking anything forcefully from anyone and remain free from jealousy. They remain independent and always deal with their friends, colleagues, and family members with love. They always tend to support and encourage love.

We all believe that parents should be highly respected and considered next to God. But first the parents must try to be the best companions and true friends of their children—such friends, who kids feel proud of and are inspired to give similar support to their own children later on. If you can prepare your kids in this manner, there cannot be a more precious gift to them.

Our kids are the future, hence it is our foremost responsibility to educate them and impart to them the wisdom about emotions. They should know that there are several ways in which emotions can be expressed. When they watch us expressing our emotions in the right manner, they will learn to do the same. So, let's take an oath to learn to express our emotions in the best and highest possible manner.

LONG-TERM EFFECTS OF PAINFUL CHILDHOOD EMOTIONS

Q. Some negative incidents had occurred in my childhood, which are still deeply embedded in my mind. I want to forget them but cannot. They cause sorrow and fear to pop up time and again. Why does this happen?

Let's assume that a little girl is traveling in a car with her mother. They meet with an accident. The girl was in the backseat and remained unharmed but her mother who was in the front seat suffered grave injuries.

So, this is the scene. The accident has occurred in the middle of the road, several people have gathered around, an ambulance arrives and the paramedics carry off the mother on a stretcher. As the girl was unhurt, she was kept away from her mother. She watches from afar her mother being taken away in the ambulance. The girl is then sent home. Since her mother was undergoing intensive and prolonged treatment at the hospital, the girl doesn't get to see her at home for many days.

After a long time, the mother recovers slightly and arrives home. She is still weak and unable to lift the little girl in her arms. The girl is noticing all of this. All these changes gradually accumulate within her. She was separated from her mother for so many days for the first time in her life.

Everything happens for the first time during childhood. For example, if someone in his childhood had tripped and fallen for the first time while crossing the road, it gets imprinted in his mind. After that, whenever he crosses the road, the feeling of tripping pops up, and all of a sudden he feels alarmed.

Something similar happened with the little girl. What she registered in her mind is: *"Something happened suddenly and my mother left me. She did not return for a long time and I had to stay without her. When she returned, she was different and did not even carry me in her arms for so many days."* This gets engraved deep within her. Now whenever she watches someone going away, the same feeling arises within her that she had encountered for the first time during her mother's accident.

This girl then grows up, gets married, and has her own kids. Now, whenever her kids go away from her, she experiences the same emotions and has a bad feeling about it. Similarly, when any of her friends bid her goodbye, she has the same uneasy feeling. When her children grow up and move elsewhere for pursuing their career, she is troubled by the same bad feeling. This means she practically lives that childhood experience for the rest of her life. Whenever she sees someone go, she feels that person is going forever and will never return. This fear is lying hidden or suppressed within her, because she was not ready for what had occurred during her childhood.

The effects of an incident appeared and left a residue within her. It is not that this was the result of her karma (actions). Sometimes some things happen that leave a residue, which gets stored permanently within the mind. On reacting to this residue, some karma occur which in turn yield their fruit. On reacting to this fruit, some more karma occur. This never-ending cycle keeps repeating. This never-ending cycle is going on in the girl's life. That is the reason why, despite becoming a mother, she is still unable to overcome the fear and grief of her childhood, and continues to experience the same emotions even now.

This is an example of just one occurrence in the life of a child. Every child faces many such incidents in their lives and they go on suppressing something in their minds. These incidents could have taken place in school, at home, in the market, sometimes with family, and sometimes with friends. Many a time, a kid is ridiculed or bullied over something, all of which gets recorded within him. He then experiences the same feeling throughout his life.

Let us consider one more example. A woman hears a song and suddenly starts feeling depressed. She wonders, "I was feeling fine some time back. Suddenly what happened that I am feeling so gloomy?"

She reflects over it and realizes that whenever she hears a certain kind of music, she feels depressed. This continued and over time it worsened to the extent that she started fearing that music and wished to avoid it. To solve this problem, she started seeing a psychiatrist. During her sessions, they came to a realization. Her mother had died when she was very young, and while her mother was being buried, that same music was playing somewhere around. Due to this, she had subconsciously associated that music with the depression she felt at that time. Therefore, now, whenever she heard that music, she would start feeling desolate.

The above example is a fact. What needs to be understood from it is that, during childhood, several such things take place which get etched in the mind and we subconsciously tend to hold on to them. We fail to understand that these things that have been recorded will no longer be useful on growing up. Yet, such programming takes place during childhood because we lack maturity and understanding at that time. We develop these qualities later as we grow up. For instance, if you look back at your childhood events now, you would see them with your present maturity and understanding, which was not possible for you in that phase of your life.

Now, it's time to change your programming. For this, you must release all the negative emotions using the methods that will be discussed later, and also you must conjoin every sad feeling with a joyful one. As soon as the seeds of joy will germinate and begin to bloom, you will automatically get rid of the effects of your old, painful programming.

THREE WAYS OF PERCEIVING EVENTS

Q. Why does every individual react differently to a given event?

Every person has had a different childhood with different experiences. An individual's personality is shaped up by the experiences that he or she has lived. This is one of the major reasons why every person is different from the other.

There is diversity everywhere in God's creation. No two flowers are the same, neither are two fruits the same, even if they belong to the same tree. Likewise, in the crowd of so many people, no two individuals are alike. These variations are not just physical but also mental and emotional. That is why, every person reacts differently to a given situation. The main reason being that each one's emotional quotient differs from the other.

Despite these differences, people can be broadly divided into three categories based on their method of perception. The first category consists of individuals who paint a picture of every event in their mind and then look at it. They can be called as 'visual' since they understand and imbibe situations better when they see them. The second category of people are those who think in words, i.e. they absorb an event by hearing it and then listen to what their mind says about it. These are 'auditory.' The third category is of those who think and understand all situations through feeling. They listen only to their feelings and are thus referred to as 'feeling' or 'kinesthetic.'

Does this mean that all individuals belong to either one of the categories? No, an individual can also be a mixture of these traits. One can be a combination of visual and auditory, or visual and feeling, or auditory and feeling. The ratio of these traits is what changes in each individual and makes him different from another. Those who belong totally to the feeling category, keep on flowing with emotions and are driven by emotions.

You may be visual, auditory, kinesthetic, or a combination, yet it is important for you to understand emotions, so that you can understand yourself as well as others and respect their feelings.

CRYING IS GOOD

Q. Is crying the same thing as being emotional? And is crying okay even after growing up?

If asked, "Are you emotional?" some people would answer "yes" and some would say "no." Many people answer this question depending on: "Do I cry a lot or not?" People often associate emotions with crying, although emotions are not always expressed through tears. There are several ways to express them.

Emotions are a part of our everyday lives, and yet we know so little of them. If we succeed in understanding them and become aware of the right way to express them, our lives will become much simpler and happier.

People think that only those who cry have emotions. This is not true, as each person has emotions within. Crying is just one way of releasing emotions. Some people release their emotions by weeping, while others by getting angry. On the other hand, some suppress their emotions and then keep falling sick. Our physical health is dependent to a large extent on our emotions.

Most people know only a few ways of releasing emotions, which provide them with just temporary relief. Often we feel despondent on encountering difficulties; and sometimes we feel low despite having everything. We then do things to distract or entertain ourselves. Unfortunately, we end up doing things which are self-deceiving in nature. Instead, at such times, we need to give ourselves some time. We need to pause. We need to stop for a few moments.

When talking to someone, if you go on speaking without taking a single pause, it will be difficult for the other person to understand what you are saying. Likewise, if you write without a single gap between words, it would be quite challenging to read and understand what you have written. That is why, a pause or a gap is crucial.

In the same way, we need a pause and a gap for ourselves too. It is essential to talk to ourselves, understand ourselves, and become our own pillar of strength. Whatever the situation or circumstance, we must not stop supporting ourselves. If you feel like crying, don't stop yourself. It is just a method of expressing your emotions and freeing yourself. Hence, let's not make negative assumptions about crying—whether it's you or others expressing in that manner. When a baby cries, we should understand that this is its method of communication.

On the other hand, there are some people who are unable to bear even a joke and start crying. Take it easy. Take a joke as a joke. Don't be sorrowful. Some people derive pleasure from being emotional and weeping. They should honestly check whether that's the case with them, and let go of that tendency. Give your tears a goal bigger than sorrow. In fact, give them a goal bigger than your biggest sorrow. Bathe in your tears and become pure and enlightened.

KNOTS OF EMOTIONS

Q. What is meant by knots of emotions? How are they formed and how can they be untangled?

Emotional knots are a direct result of negativity lying suppressed in our subconscious mind. Whenever we hear about someone's accident or illness, numerous negative thoughts run through our mind. Whenever we need to prove ourselves in a particular field, the stress gives rise to fear. If someone else achieves the position or the object that we desired, sorrow and jealousy emerge in our mind. The feeling of greed may also step in because we wish to fulfil that desire. In this way, several thoughts arise, which are accompanied by several emotions. One emotion gives rise to another and soon there is a crowd. These emotions start getting entangled with each other, forming a knot. If these emotions are not expressed, they get suppressed in the subconscious mind.

If you wish to untie these knots, you must keep yourself open. To do so, you must breathe deeply. Have you ever noticed that whenever we experience an intense emotion, our breathing changes? Our emotional health is deeply connected to our breath. Therefore, whenever a strong emotion begins to overpower you, focus your attention on your breath. Inhale and exhale deeply. You will soon experience that the intensity of the emotion is reducing.

When we receive some sad or shocking news, we often hold our breath. We watch a shocking event holding our breath. Breath infuses the body with life-energy and vitalizes the mind and body. Whenever we hold our breath, both our body and mind get constricted. Hence, you must always pay attention to your breath and breathe deeply and openly.

An open mind is ready to accept situations. It can comprehend, that whatever happened and whatever is happening, is not permanent by nature. It is going to pass. Just like how clouds gather and then pass away. No situation is permanent. Everything undergoes a change and an open mind is ready to accept changes, because such a mind is fluid and free-flowing. Stains or residues of emotions are not left on a fluid mind. It always stays clean and clear.

We teach children the importance of cleanliness. Washing hands before eating, showering daily, keeping nails clean, brushing teeth… what if we train them to also keep their mind clean? They would then never get trapped by emotions or cause harm to themselves.

Emotions are the identity of a human being. If it's a human, emotions and feelings will naturally exist. Most importantly, emotions are the main reason behind most of the things we do. They can be instrumental for our progress. But it's not okay when we are unable to curb our feelings, which then control us, taking us away from our desired goal.

It's fine if a cricketer enters the field with the feeling "I must play to win this match for my country." However, if a player from the other team says something offensive to him and he loses his temper, then his game will suffer. If he wants to play well, then he must ignore those offensive words as well as his anger. He needs to focus only on his feeling of making his country proud by winning the match.

QUESTION 9

BODY, MIND, AND FEELINGS

Q. What is the relation between the body and feelings? How can we keep our mind healthy which is ravaged by emotions?

You must not drift away in the flow of feelings. Feelings are like a part of your body. Nonetheless, you must not link them to your body. When there is a feeling of tiredness, people often think their level of consciousness has gone down. The reality is there is no connection between tiredness of the body and level of consciousness. However tired or ill a body may be, it can still maintain a higher consciousness. The level of consciousness falls due to ignorance. Despite the body being healthy and energetic, if the individual is ignorant, his level of consciousness will be low.

You must view the body and feelings from a different point of view. You must watch them just as a witness. From a distance, you should observe emotions, analyze them, evaluate them, and then decide which ones to keep and which ones to discard. If the unwanted feelings are not released but are repressed, they give rise to disorders of the mind. The repressed emotions keep on troubling the mind. Such a disturbed and unhealthy mind cannot take the body towards progress.

A child is given various tonics to keep him healthy. Along with these tonics, give him the tonic of love too. These days, various supplements and tonics are used to prevent illnesses. To remedy the ailments of the mind caused by emotions, we should always keep with us a tonic—the tonic of love. Love is a tonic that can mend all the wounds and clean the mind. It prepares the mind to accept changes. That is why, love should be awakened in the mind. This is a revolution. Revolution of calling upon love, revolution of wisdom.

RESPONDING TO ANGER

Q. How should we respond to anger—our own and that of others?

You can't take back a bullet fired,
once it's left the gun.
So too, cruel words that leave your mouth;
so try to hold your tongue.

These words contain the truth. The deepest physical wound can heal with time but the wounds caused by words are difficult to heal. Therefore, it is critical to understand others' emotions as well as to verbalize your emotions in the right manner. The art of seeing one's emotions with the right perspective is a boon for some people, while it is the greatest boon for some others, because the right understanding of emotions is the basis for a happy life.

Every human being's life is like a boat sailing in the ocean of emotions. Sometimes, the waves of this ocean are like a vehement serpent that hisses ferociously and breaks down the strongest cliffs. While, at other times, they are like a soft melody that leaves a delightful tune in our hearts. Indeed, emotions are like waves that sometimes create great turbulence in life and at other times a tickling joy. So, are we dancing to the tune of these emotions? Do our emotions rule us? Are we their slaves?

This actually depends on what we desire; do we wish to be their slaves or their master? We just need to learn how to express our emotions and how should our perspective be towards others' emotions.

In some movies, we may have seen that there is a huge robot. Although it looks gigantic, it is controlled by a relatively tiny human being, who manages its controls on the computer, and then we see the robot moving and functioning accordingly. The robot smashes and destroys things, and looks like a monster. You may have seen such scenes in movies.

An angry individual is in a similar state; hurling and shattering objects like a demon, but small and scared from within. He is actually trying to release his fear.

Whatever the outer scene may look like, when you understand yourself, you can understand others too. This knowledge will be useful for you when someone is angry and yelling at you; be it your dad, mom, neighbor, boss, mother-in-law, or anyone else. If you can give love to yourself, you will be able to give it to others too. Are you able to give love to yourself in such situations? If you can, then you are able to understand others.

We get incensed by someone's words or actions and tend to lose control. In such situations, we may utter some harsh words. People then take those words literally and hold onto them, because all they can see is the words, not the feeling or the intention behind them.

Let's consider an anecdote.

> A teacher told her student, "I will ask you a question, and you have to answer promptly. Now tell me, what is the capital of India?"
>
> The student at once replied, "Promptly."

The student was only following instructions—to the tee! This is an example to illustrate that often we focus only on words and get stuck in their web.

In order to avoid getting hurt and to save our relationships from breaking, it is vital to learn the art of expressing our emotions.

For example, **"I did not feel bad about what you said and did yesterday, but I did not feel good either. However, it's not your fault that I feel this way."**

Whoever understands the above words or is able to read in between the lines, has understood the secret of high IQ as well as EQ.

We will know the effect of these words, once we use them. We must learn the language of expressing our emotions, because if expressed wrongly, it can totally change the meaning of what we intend to say. It is necessary to express what we have not liked about someone, but most people don't want to hear about their mistakes. They are not able to bear the bitter truth. The minute you point out what you did not like, friendship turns into enmity. We must express our emotions, but equally important is what words should be used.

"I did not feel bad about what you said and did yesterday, but I did not feel good either. However, it's not your fault that I feel this way."

This sentence comprises of words, and what we speak in anger are also words. Displeasure is present in our words and so also in the above line. Emotions must be expressed, but in a way that others' emotions are not aggravated.

In a survey, people were asked about which emotion they felt assaulted by the most? Which emotion is the most difficult to deal with? Number one came out to be anger, followed by sadness, fear, worry, jealousy, guilt, and so forth. If we are overwhelmed by an emotion, what kind of response would we give? It will never be the right one. People who are equipped with emotional intelligence know ways of handling themselves during trying situations. They always remain balanced. Such people don't just succeed but are also able to stay at the peak of success. It is difficult to achieve success, and even more difficult to remain successful. This is only possible when a person understands emotional intelligence and applies it in one's daily life. Thus, emotional maturity is a must to maintain success. People attend various trainings, take medicines, attend workshops and seminars, to enhance their intellectual level. They spend ample time and money on it. But the important thing is to learn to express ourselves in the right manner.

ANGER IS A MASK

Q. What are the various ways of expressing anger, and what's the best way?

When there is optimal rain, it causes life to spring everywhere. The raindrops cool the scorched earth and germinate the seeds lying within, leading to abundant creation. However, if the same rain is excess or scanty, it can lead to disastrous effects. The same is true with emotions.

Many a time, we burst out on someone when we are angry. We pour out all our suppressed anger. We believe that by doing so, we will feel better and at peace. But what about the person on whom we exploded? When we unleash our fury upon someone, we are not just hurting that person but also ourselves. Bondage of karma is created and both get tied by it. If, of the two, even one of us is mature, the tension created by the bondage can be reduced. In fact, a mature person will not burst out on anyone. He will dissolve his feeling of anger right away. He will not allow any bondage of karma to be created. On the other hand, if the person who is bearing the outburst is mature, then he will understand the feeling of the other person. He will forgive at once and prevent himself from getting bound by the shackles of karma.

That is why, every home should have at least one mature person, who can give the outpour of emotions occurring in the household an appropriate direction. If a child in the house is shrieking and bawling his eyes out, instead of getting mad and trying to shut him up right away, wait for some time. Give him a chance to settle down by himself, as he is trying to release his anger. Do the same with adults too. If there is a downpour of anger, sit with an open umbrella—the umbrella of love. Communicate with everyone in a peaceful manner. Only by doing so, it's possible to create an atmosphere of peace at home.

So, there are two main ways in which anger is expressed. First is that of straightforward people who shout and scream at the other person. The second way is that of people who keep their emotions within and are unable to express their anger. Both ways prove to be unfavorable. Relations fall apart in case of straightforward people and the body falls sick in those who suppress emotions within.

Some people reduce their stress by talking or cursing, while some others by pushing it deep within themselves.

When a person is angry, he is actually fearful from within. Anger is like a mask that hides the real feeling. Today, maximum people suffer emotional attacks related to anger. Anger is a mask that conceals feelings like weakness, helplessness, not getting one's way, and ego.

For instance, a little girl demands a new school bag and a new pair of shoes from her father. The father cannot meet her demands because it's end of the month and he does not have the required amount. He silences the girl by rebuking her with anger. It is his helplessness due to which he cannot provide his daughter, but he does not have the courage to reveal the truth to his child. He feels embarrassed or ashamed to do so. He considers the feeling of helplessness as something bad and thereby masks it with anger. This is totally wrong. By behaving in this manner, he gave more importance to anger than to helplessness. This happens because people do not consider anger to be a sign of weakness.

It is a common misconception that people who express anger are the stronger ones and those who express helplessness are weak. No one wishes to appear weak and hence they use rage to cover their helplessness. In such cases, one should contemplate with honesty upon certain questions: "What is happening within me when I am expressing anger? What I am trying to hide is getting accumulated within me and eating away at me. Then what's the right thing to do?"

The right thing to do is facing the truth, speaking the truth, talking honestly with yourself, behaving honestly with your family, and directing your emotions by understanding them. Only these steps can help you achieve a healthy body and mind. Blowing up in anger and suppressing anger, both are wrong. You must be free of both and use the method of 'emotionless communication.'

EMOTIONLESS COMMUNICATION FOR EMOTIONAL MATURITY

Q. What is emotionless communication?

It means communicating without getting carried away by emotions. The scope of communication is huge and widespread. Most often, problems crop up in communication because people add their emotions to it. This reduces the clarity of their communication and the other person is unable to understand their message.

Like someone says, "You should have kept this thing here, but you have kept it over there." This is a very simple communication, which has no emotion coupled with it. It only spells out what is the right place of that object. However, when emotions are combined to this communication, it sounds something like, "Do you even realize how much trouble you have caused by placing this thing here?!"

Emotions creep into communication when you have previously created some tales in your mind about something, and they get activated within you in the current situation. Otherwise, it is just a simple communication. If it was done via email or texting, the chances of emotions joining in would be minimal. When you are speaking to someone, the tone in your voice tends to communicate your emotion. You only need to pay attention to that tone. Always remember that whatever you need to communicate with anyone, you must do it without adding any emotions to it.

You will then be able to communicate just the plain facts, such as, "This object must be kept at this particular spot only. This is its place. And if placed here, everyone will be able to find it easily." However, if you say, "By keeping this object at the wrong place, you have caused such hassle, wasted so much time, delayed so many other activities…," then you are narrating the tale made up in your mind.

Likewise, there is one more common tale that people often create like, "By placing this thing here, you have proved how careless you are." Whether that person is really careless or is your own mirror, will be proved later on, but for now, you must clearly recognize: "I am adding my emotion to this incident and narrating my own made-up tale." After identifying this, you will communicate without adjoining any emotion. This is known as emotionless communication.

If you learn this art of communication, you will not be swept up by emotions and will be known as an emotionally mature person.

DEALING WITH PAINFUL EMOTIONS

Q. How should we deal with painful emotions?

Often, people stand in a long queue to buy suffering. This means they suffer even when they need not. In fact, they proactively approach sorrow. It's like someone purchasing tickets in black for not just a tax-free movie but for a totally free movie. This happens due to ignorance and unconsciousness. People hold on to suffering due to ignorance. They don't remember who they actually are. They forget that they are not the body, they are the infinite Consciousness or the cinema screen, that does not get affected in any way by the emotions of the actors or the environment in the movie. Only the body and mind get affected by sorrow.

This situation is just like someone assumes a rope to be a snake and lives his entire life with that belief. The one, who realizes that it is not a snake but a rope, is liberated from the suffering as well as the sufferer (the individual ego which thinks *I am suffering*). You will attain this liberation only when you realize and experience your true self, which is called Self Realization. Just like the cinema screen is not impacted by rain or shine in the movie, similarly your true self is not affected by any suffering or hardship in your life.

It is natural for emotions to arise in the mind; however, if they stay stuck in the mind, then it's an ailment. Gradually, these emotions get entrenched in the mind, and whenever they get the opportunity, they surface and cause suffering. This is dangerous.

Every first incidence that takes place in our life leaves its impression upon us. Whenever we are faced with a situation for the first time, its impact is deep. For example, an individual fails his first ever interview due to some difficult questions asked by the interviewer. Fear of interviews will now take root in his mind. Every time he will wonder, "Can I face the interview? What questions will they ask?!"

Suppose you get a call in the middle of the night, informing you about your relative's hospitalization or demise. Thereafter, whenever you get a late night call, you feel scared. The feeling that was buried in your mind surfaces once again. This means the first experience got recorded in your subconscious and the fear took hold within.

Once bitten twice shy. This happens because of the ingrained fear of being bitten. The event gets associated with the feeling and forms a knot in your mind. These emotional knots suddenly come to the fore with similar situations and launch an emotional attack. Whenever any event occurs, be it small or big, it triggers the assault of all similar old and new events, leading to a phase of despair. In situations like these, sometimes you wonder, "Why am I feeling so unhappy over such a minor incident? Why such irritation?"

The reason for the unhappiness and irritation is not that single event. The reason is the opening of the older knots of emotions or awakening of those old buried emotions. The old and the new emotions together cause suffering.

There are several types of emotions, but there are two main types. The first are minor emotions. For example, someone tells you, "Don't talk to me" or "Don't scold me." These are not big enough issues to cause you to lose control of your emotions. If the issue was not that substantial, then why did anger arise within you? That's because similar incidents had taken place in your past too. The current event simply triggered open the old emotional knots.

However, many emotions are not even real. For example, you get frightened when you assume a rope to be a snake. This happens because actually the fear of snakes is already entrenched in your mind and it surfaces because a rope looks similar to a snake. Suppose, it's dark and you notice a rope lying beneath your pillow. You think it's a snake and yelp. You are sweating with fear and your heart is pounding against your chest. The question is, was there any real basis for your reaction? No. These are pseudo emotions. This is the second main type of emotion.

The events that take place in our lives teach us an important lesson: Whenever any emotion arises within you, neither get swept away by it nor support it. Nonetheless, both these things happen when we consider a belief embedded in our mind to be the truth. Not just the truth, but the irrefutable truth. For instance, we often say with total conviction: "He never listens to me, never does what I tell him to, never pays attention to me… Nobody helps me or supports me…" Have you ever thought that the few people who do not support you are not really the whole world? Life is connected to many people and many circumstances. Most of them have supported you, although you may not have noticed or been aware of. Even the environment and nature supports us every step of the way; however, we ignore that and instead always complain of nobody helping us. From where do we get the oxygen that we breathe? Aren't the trees supporting us? The ground that we walk on, isn't it supporting us? Yet we are plagued by the thought that nobody is helping us. There are so many things that are aiding you so you can read this book, for example, a chair, your eyes, your glasses, your hands, the publisher, and so on.

The reality is that the whole universe is helping us at every step, at every breath, and every moment. However, we never pay attention to it. We are so engrossed in backing our own negative emotions that we do not understand the value of the service we are receiving. At such times, it is crucial to witness our unhappy emotions and release them with the right understanding. Let's understand how this can be done.

Let's assume that your unhappy emotion is colorless. Now mix your favorite color in it and visualize that color at the spot where you experience that emotion—for example, in your chest. By doing this, you will feel lightness or even happiness or a neutral feeling in that area. You can read all the steps given below and then try this experiment.

1. Close your eyes and be seated in a posture of your choice.
2. Now observe and check where are you experiencing the unhappy feeling in your body. Locate that spot.
3. Once you locate it, visualize your favorite color mixing with the colorless unhappy feeling, just like in a mixer.
4. As the color continues to merge into the colorless, the colorless ceases to exist. You are being colored by your favorite color—the color of happiness.

5. When your feelings are colored by happiness, watch the miracle of how the power of the painful feelings diminishes and how you are shifting from negative to positive.

Whenever distressing emotions overpower you, whether of grief, rejection, heartbreak, failure, fear, or anything else, try this experiment. You must do this for yourself, so that you can be free from every kind of suffering. The rest you will anyways receive as a bonus. You only need to decide: "I am going to keep myself happy." The feeling of happiness will work like a magnet and attract all the good things into your life.

SORROW RELATED TO EVENTS

Q. How can we attain freedom from sorrow related to certain events?

It is easy to be free from sorrow which is attached to events. For this, we need to understand how the mind experiences an event.

Your mind experiences any event according to your level of consciousness at that time. If your consciousness level is low, your mind may believe the event to be true and feel miserable. If your level is high, your mind will feel happy. If you are able to clearly see this drama of the mind, your sufferings will stop. Proceed with this understanding and also continue to reflect on it. The more you reflect, the more clarity you gain. With clarity, your happiness level goes up. You will eventually not give much importance to anything that causes sorrow in your life.

You feel sorrow only when you get attached to an event. So, if you are feeling sorrow, take it as normal instead of regarding it as a problem. It becomes a problem when you keep a part of that sorrow within you, by clinging to it and constantly brooding over it. The better option would be to find the reason behind your sorrow and search for its solution.

Let's consider an analogy.

> While watching a movie in a theater, we see the movie playing on a screen. We very well know that we are separate from the movie. However, let's suppose that if we cut a piece of that screen and keep it with us, we would feel ourselves to be a part of that movie. Until that piece of the screen is with us, we will feel attached to the movie. As soon as we reattach the piece to the screen, we will once again feel separate from the movie.

It is the same with any problem or suffering. "Why has this difficulty or sorrow appeared in *my* life?" When we think in this manner, it is like keeping that piece of screen with you. As soon as you release this thought, you are able to witness your suffering with detachment. This is what needs to be done. Watch your sorrow or problem as if it is playing on a screen in front of you. This will take them into the background, away from you. Due to this, you are able to see them clearly, because now they are not right in your face. You can see the whole picture. Thereby, you start seeing the solution to your problem and begin to feel free from it.

Henceforth, whenever any adversity or pain appears, all you have to do is take them to the background and separate yourself from that background. In this way, you will put your suffering at its right place instead of keeping it in your pocket. Then, if possible, search for the solution to the problem to get rid of it. You will not just feel free, but also achieve detachment from the sufferings associated with your body.

DISTRESS ON SEEING OTHERS SUFFER

Q. I feel distressed when I see others in misery. I cannot bear it; what should I do about it?

There are many people who suffer on seeing others in suffering. And they think it's impossible to be free from this tendency called *emotional empathy*. But it is possible.

If you think that you should not feel miserable on seeing the misery of others, then you are right. When you feel upset by others' sorrow, it is because of your sensitive nature, which is a good quality. If you are happy because of others' happiness and feel sad due to their sadness, it means you are able to experience *oneness*. The problem arises when your sensitivity is devoid of wisdom, because that causes you pain. It's just like a bird can fly high only when it has the support of both its wings. You have the wing of sensitivity but not the other wing of wisdom. Sensitivity is already dominant in you. You must, however, look at it in a positive way.

People who are emotional by nature, believe their sensitivity to be the reason for most of their problems. They believe that people emotionally blackmail them and take advantage of them by making an emotional fool out of them. In reality, all of this happens due to lack of wisdom. If they lack wisdom, they cannot fly high, because essentially they are lacking the second wing. No one can make an emotional fool out of you if you have wisdom. When you are wise, suffering cannot make you suffer. That's because you understand that your suffering is not going to help the other person who is in misery; however, your happiness can help in reducing their misery. When someone is in pain and you look at them through the eyes of love and joy, there will be an improvement in their state.

A patient feels much better just at the sight of a doctor. Is this because the doctor cries or feels sad or falls sick for him? No. The first thing the doctor does is tell the patient, "It's alright. Don't worry. You'll get well soon." Then he begins his examination and treatment. Just the look in his eyes can bring an improvement in the patient because his presence is reassuring, which conveys, "This is not such a big deal, your illness can be easily cured." The doctor's knowledge or wisdom itself works like a medicine on the patient. The more the doctor is knowledgeable and capable, the faster the patient improves. When the patient sees the look of "No big deal, you will get well soon," in the eyes of the doctor, he starts believing in his quick recovery.

This is why you must check what are your eyes filled with? Joy or sorrow? Are they filled with suffering or happiness? There is no problem if you feel others' pain as your pain, because only such people search for ways to liberate others from their suffering.

But this is possible only when others' sorrow spurs you on to do something constructive about it; when it becomes your strength. If their pain is causing you pain and illness, then you need to work on yourself. The better option is to learn the art of remaining happy even during sorrow. You become a magnet when you are happy, which attracts the best and highest solutions. The opposite is also true when you are upset and miserable. Hence, your eye should be such that it turns you into a magnet. From now on, whenever you notice someone in pain, remind yourself that your presence must be positive and joyful. Also count your blessings at such times. Your presence will then bring improvement in the condition of the sorrowful individual or the patient.

In reality, you wish to free others from pain by experiencing their pain. However, if your suffering is becoming a hurdle in liberating them of their suffering, common sense dictates that first *you* must be free from your sorrow. In order to do so, you can recall the happy incidents that have occurred in your life, or bring forth your pleasant memories. And thank the universe for them. There are so many things in every person's life which can give him happiness. The truth is that happiness resides within us. That is why, as soon as you remind yourself of it, you will feel happy. You will then look at the other person through the eyes of bliss, and speak words of encouragement, which will improve his condition.

When someone is sad, he often expects his family and close ones to feel the same. Otherwise, he doesn't believe they love him. If it's so important for him that you should look sad, then you will have to pretend to be sad, so that he believes you love him. But if you wish to improve his state, then you must tell yourself, "I must first come out of my suffering." Feeling sad because of another's sadness indicates that although one of your wing is strong, the other is weak. That's why you must now strengthen it, so that you can fly high.

QUESTION 16

FEELING OF INSECURITY OR INCAPABILITY

Q. I feel I am incapable of doing some things, which are actually not very difficult. What can be the reason?

To tame an elephant, only one of its legs is tied up with a chain when it's just a baby. The baby elephant tries to free itself many times, but is unable to, due to lack of strength. When it grows up, it can break the chain, but does not even attempt to, as it continues to believe that it cannot get free. It stops trying for the rest of its life because of its belief: "This chain is too strong and I cannot break it." Although the reality is that shattering a chain is no big deal for an adult elephant.

The same happens with man. He believes his childhood programming to be the truth even after growing up. For example, a person had tried to lift a weight of 10 kg in his childhood but was unable to do so. On growing up, he believes the same thing to be true, and says, "This is too heavy; I cannot lift it." He should be told, "You have grown up now. Have a look at yourself in the mirror. As a child, you may have found a weight of 10 kg to be heavy. But that was then. The same is not true at present."

If some other creature thinks it is incapable and behaves accordingly, it can be excused, because it may not have the required level of intelligence and understanding. But when a human being behaves in this manner, he must be imparted knowledge.

It is critical to reflect once more on: *How much power do others' words and the thoughts of others and your own hold? Are they powerful enough to cause you pain?* You felt the impact of those words and assumptions much more when you were a child, because you were emotionally naïve at that time. But now you have grown and your emotional strength has increased manifold.

The reality is the strength of thoughts is lesser than that of a mosquito. But you constantly nurture your thoughts, making them powerful.

Until a thought has attacked, you are relaxed and may be even humming a tune. The moment a negative thought or a bad feeling appears, everything changes—for the worse. For instance, a thought appears in someone's mind: "I am ill, I am getting old, and I cannot continue this work anymore." What happens then?

Let's assume that you have some appliances and gadgets in your house. Some of them may be old and not in top shape, but they still work quite okay. This is because they do not have a mind that says: "I am ill, I am weak, how will I do this work?" You may still be cooking in the same old pots and pans, and the food would still be tasting good. The food never tastes bad due to those utensils. You use them daily and yet they play their role quite well.

The same does not happen with man, most of the times. His subconscious mind is triggered by a thought, due to which he begins to feel: *I am old and sick; how will I do this?*

It's just like someone is leading a happy life and then suddenly out of the blue is assailed by a thought: "What if my medical reports detect cancer?" This one thought disperses all his joy and he is enveloped in misery.

Your subconscious mind keeps whispering various tales in your ear. Like when a relative tells you repeatedly about a certain individual: "He's not a good person. He is actually very bad." When you meet the individual you were told about, you tend to look at him with judgment. You consider him to be bad, no matter how he is. This happens because when your relative told you the same thing repeatedly, your subconscious mind recorded it. When you met that individual, the subconscious whispered what it had recorded. You believe it and so you are unable to understand *your* judgment and *your* feelings clearly about that individual.

Later, when you come across a book on this subject, you realize the truth about feelings and start getting liberated from the whisperings and judgments of the subconscious mind. After that, you start cleansing your subconscious.

In childhood, the subconscious mind proclaims: "This chain is too strong." Due to this, the baby elephant does not try to break free from the chain even after growing up. People who train elephants or other big animals are aware of this particular weakness. They know that unlike the way human intelligence evolves over time, animals have not evolved in the same manner since ages. If intelligence would have developed further in elephants, their inner growth would have begun. This is because if awakening takes place in any one of them, it would follow in others as well. This is nature's law, but for this to happen, awakening in at least one is necessary. The reality is that the possibility of awakening exists only in humans. Only a human being can be told and expected to understand that, "You consider yourself weak only because your subconscious mind has announced this to you, but actually it is not the truth."

We believe so many things in our mind, like, life is tough in this world, it is difficult to understand people, everything is so much more difficult in these times, there is a lot of competition today which did not exist earlier, and so on.

Stuck in this web of beliefs created by the subconscious, we declare: "I won't be able to break the chains of these beliefs; I have tried a lot but failed," or "I cannot get rid of my sorrow; I tried so much." What we don't realize is that this declaration is hollow. We need to be told, "Now you have grown up. Even though it was not possible for you earlier, you are now equipped with emotional strength that makes everything possible. Come out of the tales spun by your subconscious. You may have sorrows in your life, but do not consider it impossible to overcome them. That would be a huge mistake."

Only a human being can be expected to break free from the chains of slavery tied by the subconscious mind. You can easily break these chains because you are now an adult. You are now gaining the knowledge of feelings and emotions, and you must let a new understanding, new courage, and new zeal build within you, which proclaims: "I will break free of all the chains that I have believed to be bound by. I will list down all the things that I feel are difficult to do and will accomplish them one by one."

When you will see the results of these actions, you will then be saying, "This was so simple... I only needed to yank the chains off with all my heart. Why did I take so much time to do this, who was stopping me?!"

It is necessary to pull at the chains with all your heart, as half-hearted efforts never yield success. Half-hearted effort means you don't actually believe in the process but merely give it a try.

Breaking free of your chains (wrong beliefs) is not a difficult task. All you need is a little bit of homework. Just like if you work daily on something, it does not seem much, but if you try to finish a year's work in a single day, then it seems too much. The same is true for the chains of suffering. If man learns to do one thing at a time, he will never feel burdened.

Every person will need to do this homework of contemplation someday; whether by himself or on being forced by someone else. The one who loves freedom will not wait and would simply get down to his homework, because he wants to be free.

To be free, you must now look at everything once again in a new way, with truth. Whatever is old and obsolete must be changed completely. As soon as you comprehend this, you suddenly grow up. Nothing remains the same. You begin to stay happy all the time. Earlier, the subconscious had put some limitations upon you due to the feeling of insecurity, but now since you have grown up, the insecurity no longer remains.

UNCOMFORTABLE FEELINGS & NEURAL PATHWAYS

Q. How should we handle uncomfortable feelings? For instance, some months back, I lost my job, and when I reached home, my house was full of guests! At my new job, I have worked hard but my colleague was applauded, not me. I took time out of my busy schedule to attend a family function, but nobody there paid any attention to me. How to deal with the feelings caused by such kind of incidents? And I was also wondering what is the connection between the brain and feelings?

We all have feelings. More often than not, what we dread are uncomfortable feelings. Let's look at some more examples along with the scenarios you mentioned in order to understand this topic comprehensively.

a. Imagine, you have been busy with lots of activities and suddenly there is no activity. How would you feel then?

b. You have been fired from work. You reach home and the house is full of guests. How would you feel then?

c. Despite you working hard, your colleague got recognition and you were not acknowledged. How would you feel?

d. On a quiet Sunday, when you are sitting at home alone, all of a sudden a sad memory from the past pops up in your mind and you become sad. What would you do then?

e. You call for a meeting and no one turns up. How would you feel?

f. One of your prospective clients calls off his business and all your future plans crumble. How would you feel?

g. You take out time from your busy schedule and go for a family function. No one attends to you there. How would you feel?

It is observed that in most of the above mentioned scenarios, one feels uncomfortable. We either shut down the emotion by suppressing it or find a temporary way of escaping it by diverting our focus to activities that provide temporary relief. One may switch on the television, call a friend, chat with someone, surf on the net, go for eating out, take a walk, express one's anger, etc. So, what happens in the brain when it comes to these uncomfortable feelings?

In everyday language, we often use the terms 'feelings' and 'emotions' interchangeably as they are closely associated with each other. We are constantly interacting with the external world through our senses. Our brain is receiving signals from the body, registering what is going on inside our body. Emotions are the complex reactions the body has to certain stimuli.

When a situation that we have associated with fear occurs, it activates various body sensations. Our heart begins to race, our mouth becomes dry, our skin turns pale, and our muscles contract. These sensations form a physical snapshot in the brain. This physical snapshot is triggered automatically and unconsciously whenever the situation is repeated. When the brain interprets the situation as one of fear, it initiates this emotional reaction that leads to the physical symptoms.

However, not all feelings result from the body's reaction to external stimuli. Sometimes, we see a sick person and empathize with him. At such times, we simulate the pain in our brain. Without actually experiencing the pain physically, we recreate that person's pain to a certain degree internally.

Sometimes, the physical snapshot is also not accurate as the brain ignores certain physical signals when the body goes through severe stress or intense fear. Thus, sometimes the brain doesn't receive the accurate snapshot of the physical state and misinterprets the feeling. At other times, even though it receives the correct snapshot, it still misinterprets the feeling. It may blow up the intensity and severity of a feeling to such an extent, as if a panic button has been pressed. At times, the entire body starts trembling with fear. If it senses an uncomfortable feeling, it tries to do away with it. It prompts the body to act in such a way that it escapes from the uncomfortable situation.

From childhood, whatever we have believed to be true is stored in our brain. These beliefs are nothing but the neural pathways which decide how the brain should interpret the emotions, which feelings should be generated, and how to respond to them. Accordingly, the brain directs the body to behave in a particular way. It's like all of them are wired together and fire together.

If the brain is faced with an emotion which doesn't match with the set belief system, then instead of reporting that it doesn't know how to interpret this emotion, it replays any of the existing feelings like anger, boredom, comparison, disgust, depression, envy, fear, guilt, hatred, ill-will, jealousy, etc. Our physical state also changes accordingly. The brain releases chemicals along the neural pathway and the symptoms appear on different parts of the body.

For every emotion, different parts of the body are affected. For instance, when the feeling of anger arises in a body, the brain releases stress hormones in the body. It shunts blood away from the gut and towards the muscles, in preparation for physical exertion. Heart rate, blood pressure, respiratory rate, and body temperature increase, and the skin perspires.

As we see it, we believe in it, and reinforce the emotion. As the brain automates these responses, you will not be consciously aware of them to take the corrective actions. At such times, instead of masking the underlying emotion, you need to fully feel it and face it. As you re-evaluate it, you understand its actual intensity. Then you need to give clear inputs to the brain on how to process this information. Thus, a new neural pathway will get formed with the renewed response.

CREATING NEW PATHWAYS IN THE BRAIN

Q. What is the practical application of the knowledge of emotions and neural pathways?

Let's understand the practical application. Whenever you experience an uncomfortable feeling, it means your brain is not able to process the information properly. You need to give correct inputs to your brain in order to harbor positive feelings such as love, joy, peace, patience, courage, compassion, and the like. Let's now revisit the scenarios that were mentioned earlier in light of this understanding.

1. If you have been busy with lots of activities and suddenly there is no activity, you may feel a void within. Your brain will interpret it as a feeling of boredom and may want to indulge in activities such as chatting, shopping, eating out, etc. At such time, understand that since you have not given correct

inputs to your brain, it's resorting to these avenues. When such feeling arises, you need to tell your brain to behave differently. You may practice meditation and become aware of the exact physical state. One of the best meditations for emotions is to watch your breath. As you focus on your breath, your breathing calms down and the effect of the emotion also reduces.

2. You have been fired from work. You reach home and the house is full of guests. At such a time, you would have loved to be by yourself. But when you see guests around, your brain doesn't understand how to interpret this feeling, and you can get frustrated and try to avoid the situation. At such times, you could have just watched your emotions and evaluated them: Are they really heavy or do they just seem to be heavy? How much do they actually weigh—5 kg or 5 g? On weighing them in your mind with detachment, you would have found that they are not as intense as they seemed. That would have helped you in being patient in that situation.

3. Despite you working hard, your colleague got recognition and you are not acknowledged. The reward center in your brain is already activated to receive the recognition. The neural pathway is triggered and you crave for appreciation. Suddenly, when you see your colleague getting all the credit, your brain interprets it as an unwelcome situation and fires anger through the neural pathway. However, you should understand that you could have given a different response. You could have chosen to rejoice in your friend's glory. By doing so, you get tuned with those positive vibrations, and some day you too will get recognized. By being angry, you get into negative vibrations.

4. On a quiet Sunday when you are sitting at home alone, all of a sudden a sad memory from the past pops up in your mind

and you become sad. At that time, you feel it's right to be sad. However, by being sad, you reinforce the seeds of sadness for your future. Instead, you can choose to be happy. By being happy, you program your brain to handle with happiness such kind of situations in the future.

5. You call for a meeting and no one turns up. You may feel furious and insulted. By feeling that way, you only torture yourself. Rather than trying to control what others should do, first control your emotions. Be patient and happy regardless of how the situation is. By being happy, you respect yourself.

6. One of your prospective clients calls off his business and all your future plans crumble. You may feel disappointed and hopeless. Your body will also start showing symptoms accordingly. However, you can still choose to accept the situation and relax. Feel yourself fully. Once the feelings subside, then with a calm mind, you can think about the best possible solution and start working on it.

7. You take time out from your busy schedule to attend a family function. But no one attends to you over there. You feel left out or ignored. You curse your decision to be there. You start thinking that instead of being there, you could have focused on completing some of your priority tasks. In this situation, ask yourself that if you were given proper attention, would such thoughts have appeared in your mind? No. So, this is the old neural pathway in your brain which is triggering this reaction. The brain has misinterpreted your emotions; hence such feeling has arisen. It was your decision to be there. The happiness you experienced while taking that decision can still continue. Your happiness is not dependent upon any external factors. With this declaration, you will feel happy.

Your happiness may attract others towards you but that's a bonus.

As you change your feelings, your brain gets rewired with the new programming and the same situations will open new doors of possibilities for you.

DIFFERENCE BETWEEN EMOTIONS AND FEELINGS

Q. What is the difference between emotions and feelings? Or are they the same?

There is a difference between emotions and feelings. Let's understand it.

An incident occurs and *emotions* arise. Then you start thinking about that incident. You think, "*This* is bad," or "That person did wrong," and you stamp on it to be absolutely true. Then you create a story about it, and start feeling sad believing that story to be true. Suppose, after feeling sad, you think, "This sorrow has arrived for my growth." How will you feel after this thought?! This is the *feeling* that the Self (your true, divine self) gives you.

On the other hand, after feeling sad if you think, "I suppose this is how it's always going to be with me…," then the unhappiness that arises is also a *feeling* sent by the Self. How's that? Let's understand. When the Self sees your negative thinking, it sends you an unhappy feeling to convey to you that what you are thinking is not correct. It tries to awaken you by sending an unhappy feeling. When the Self is trying to awaken you, it's a *feeling*. When the mind is being sad, it's an *emotion*. That's the difference between the two.

As soon as an incident occurs, tell yourself, "This incident is reminding me what kind of life I want. I want a life in which positive events take place, not negative." The Self approves of this thought, and immediately gives you a pat on the back in the form of a happy feeling. With this happy feeling, the Self is telling you, "You are on the right track. Keep it up!"

By remaining in the feeling of Self, you will be inspired to take the right action in response to an event. This will lead to the creation of new neural pathways in your brain in place of the old ones. You will thereby start achieving freedom from the burden of negative emotions.

EVERLASTING PEACE AND JOY

Q. What is the message for the youth, since they usually experience the most intense emotions and get swept up by them? Plus, how can we attain freedom from the vagaries of emotions, and experience everlasting peace, joy, and contentment? And, most importantly, what is the ultimate purpose of our life and how can we achieve it?

Deep and everlasting peace, joy, and contentment are not something that can be bought from the market. It's a feeling that can be experienced only when we have clarity and conviction of "Who am I? Why am I on this Earth?"

Realizing our true divine self (Self Realization), abiding in it permanently (Self Stabilization), and expressing its divine qualities (Self Expression) is the ultimate purpose of our life on Earth.

Swami Vivekananda, in his short life span, spread the great spiritual philosophy of India throughout the world. His thoughts and philosophy of non-duality and oneness were accepted even by his opponents. This was all possible due to his strong faith and inner strength. His message to all, especially the youth, was also the same: "Let your strength never decrease. Don't be weak. Whenever your strength goes down, your vision for your goal will start fading. To boost your power, you must increase your inner strength and spiritual strength."

Swami Vivekananda's life is an example of inner strength and conviction. The word 'Swami' means one who is the master of his emotions. The one who can control his emotions is the one who can bring clarity and conviction in his thoughts.

Youth are the present and the future, but youth is also a state in which one should be aware of why they are on Earth and what is the purpose of their life? Thus, the youth must muster strength as soon as they feel weak. Wherever and whenever their strength diminishes, they must take steps. When they feel that their self-confidence and strength is low, they must focus on listening discourses on Supreme Truth, reading books on Truth, contemplating it, and practicing meditation. This applies to not just the youth, but to everyone. Each of us has to develop conviction and clarity in our thoughts. To increase our inner strength, we must ask ourselves a few small but clear questions:

First question: What is the body?

The body is a vehicle to help us achieve our purpose on Earth.

We live all our life believing ourselves to the body. All our joys and sorrows, desires and decisions, are based on this belief. But the supreme truth is: You are not the body. The body is your vehicle. You say, "My car, my motorcycle, my body…" When you say "my" it means that object is outside of you, it is not you. Just as your car or motorcycle is not you, in the same way, your body is not you. You consider your body to be you because of wrong programming since childhood by people around you, who in turn were wrongly programmed since their childhood. This is part of the cosmic illusion (*maya*) and divine game (*leela*).

The real you is formless and infinite. The human body is a wonderful instrument created for experiencing and expressing your true self. However, our body has the tendency of getting shaken a bit by the emotions that arise in the mind. What do we do then? Just like we do not stop driving our car if it shudders a bit intermittently, likewise, we must not get disturbed by the emotions that come and go. We must continue to train our body to achieve our ultimate purpose on Earth. That's the approach we should have towards our body.

Second question: What is the mind?

Just like every part of the body is important, the mind also has its importance. But what's more crucial is that the mind should be clean and pure. The mind and body are deeply connected to each other. The mind stays connected to the body from birth till death.

On birth, the mind is good—pure, clean, like a cool fire. A cool fire is one which does not emit smoke when fuel is poured into it. Here, fuel signifies the experiences of our five senses. Experiences gained during childhood are pure and simple in nature. They are free from envy, anger, hatred, and other negative tendencies. Hence, this mind is called as the good mind.

As we start growing up, this good mind starts becoming bad, i.e. it becomes the *contrast mind*. It's this mind that contrasts, compares, and judges good and bad in everything. Which lives in the past, always mulling over what happened in the past and why, and what will happen in the future. With the help of emotional intelligence, we must convert this contrast mind into a clean mind—that which is cleansed and made pure by forgiveness. A mind that is free from anger, jealousy, malice, and other negative tendencies. How? Let us understand this.

The mind is more interested in thinking than feeling, because it does not like the present feeling. That is why, it loves to think and create tales in the brain: *"That man intentionally behaves like this... he hates me... thinks too high of himself."* It's not certain whether that man really thinks too high of himself or not; it's just a made-up story. Instead of spinning yarn in this manner, we should tell ourself, "I am now becoming emotionally mature. It's not necessary to say such things. There is no need to agonize myself by thinking in this way."

Let's consider another incident. A person complains, "I asked her to switch on the fan and yet she did not. She's just not bothered and doesn't care at all. She doesn't do what I tell her... all this means she hates me." The person doesn't realize that there can be ten different reasons for her not switching on the fan. If he talks to her, he may realize that she had not heard him at all or probably switched on something else because she misheard him.

The fact of the matter is: she did not switch on the fan because she did not. It's that simple. There is no particular meaning or story behind it. But the mind tends to blabber. *"Now she has realized her mistake, she is feeling guilty, that's why now she has turned the fan* on… or maybe it's because she herself is feeling hot… She always does this. She never does anything when asked to, but does it later on when she feels like it. She simply wants to irritate me."What happens by thinking in this manner? You sometimes feel up and sometimes down. Sometimes good and sometimes bad. Amidst all of this, you miss out on smiling and living the right way. You miss out on happiness.

She did not do it because she did not do it. She did it later because she did it later. This is the only reason and only meaning behind it, and nothing else. You will stay happy if you don't try to derive the meaning from everything a person does. But if you still wish to, at least don't derive such meanings that cause you misery. This thought is of a matured mind. If you wish to find meanings, why not try to find the meaning behind all good things in the world? You will enjoy it. Praise the Creator and you will find happiness springing in your heart.

Why and when does the good mind become the bad mind?

The good mind becomes the bad mind when our senses pour the wrong fuel into our cool flame, thereby creating smoke. When our eyes, ears, nose, tongue, and skin, transmit wrong experiences to the mind. These senses gather the wrong fuel from their surroundings. Wrong fuel is derived from wrong beliefs and notions, ignorance, superstitions, and the like. These are the cause of the smoke.

For example, a child grows up listening to numerous superstitious beliefs such as: *If a cat crosses your path, something bad will happen. If your palm is itching, you are going to receive money. If your eye is twitching, it's a bad omen.* The child did not know any of this and had a clean slate when he was born. He grows up listening to these tales, which start taking root in his mind. These misbeliefs reach him through various sources—friends, teachers, society, media, films, politics, etc. Consequently, the good mind becomes bad and starts emitting smoke.

The smoke is symbolic of the tendencies and vices of our mind, which lead us on to bad habits and addictions. These create a fog around the mind. We must learn to stop the bad fuel from getting within us. During meditation, we halt all our senses, thus also halting any fuel from going in; but this does not happen at other times. When all our senses pour wrong experiences into our mind, a heavy fog engulfs it, making us incapable of seeing anything clearly. At such times, it is essential to clear away the fog of our vices, only then can we see our goal clearly.

Unconsciously, almost every individual has set the same goal: Satisfying the Senses. Not only have people made this their goal, but they also constantly live it. This is the cause of the smoke, the cause of the pure mind turning impure. Until this fog disperses, you will not be able to see or realize your ultimate goal on Earth. That is why, it is necessary to meditate every day for at least 10-15 minutes. You can increase one minute each year. Initially, you may not be able to concentrate. You may feel that nothing is happening and there is no result. But you must continue despite these feelings and then you will begin to see its results. The fog will start receding and you will begin to know what the mind is.

Third question: What is the Self?

When there is fire, storm, or water shown on a movie screen, the screen neither burns, nor gets wet, or damaged by the storm. A similar screen is within us too, which no vice or defilement can touch. All the games of the mind, fire, smoke, fog, everything is going on upon the screen, yet the screen remains unaffected. This is the Self, our true self, the Supreme Consciousness, which is divine, formless, and limitless.

Realizing our true self is known as Self Realization or Experience of the Self. In this state, we not only get rid of suffering but also from the sufferer. We become free of the individual ego that makes us believe we are separate from the Creator and the rest of creation. We experience oneness and bliss.

We can get established in our true self (Self Stabilization) with the help of spiritual wisdom, spiritual practice, and divine devotion. With stabilization, we attain the state of permanent joy, love, peace, and contentment—which are basically our intrinsic divine qualities. Thereafter, what remains is the expression of these and other innate divine attributes. This is how we can achieve the ultimate purpose of our life.

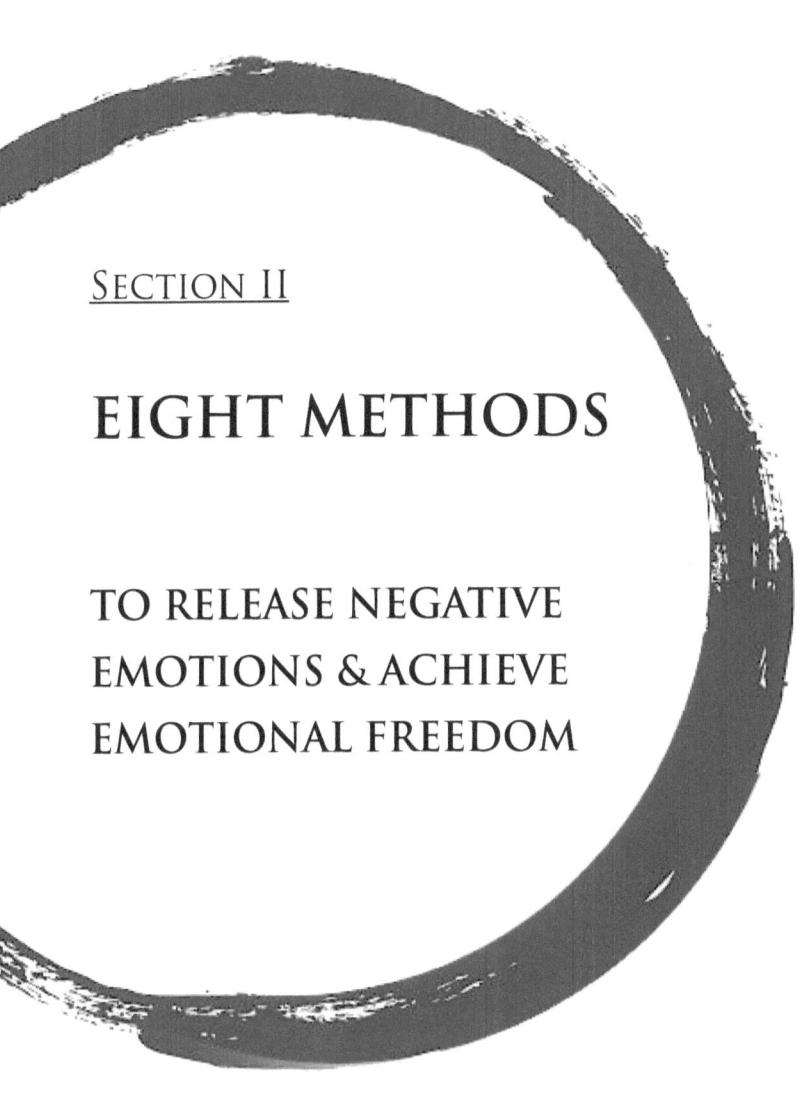

Section II

EIGHT METHODS

TO RELEASE NEGATIVE EMOTIONS & ACHIEVE EMOTIONAL FREEDOM

HOW TO ATTAIN EMOTIONAL FREEDOM
Play with your emotions

Often people's life gets stuck on that one person who did not help them. That's it. The thought, *"Nobody helps me or supports me; I have to do everything by myself,"* gets impressed upon their mind. This thought troubles them a lot. However, one must honestly reflect upon whether there really is any truth in that notion.

The reality is we receive unconditional support from so many factors due to which we are able to live and function. The process of breathing to keep us alive occurs on its own, without any effort from our side. Air, water, sunlight, etc. that are essential for our existence, are provided by nature freely and abundantly. Thus, we receive ample support from all directions, but we tend to feel unhappy about things we haven't received and do not value those that we have. Hence, whenever you get the thought, "I have to do everything on my own," take a little pause and ponder a while.

Untrue thoughts and emotions such as the above will continue to appear in our minds. What we must decide is to not take their side. In the beginning, the mind will revolt, but stay determined to not entertain those emotions. This habit will stop the spiral of negative emotions that take you down. This will mark the beginning of your journey to emotional freedom.

Emotions will try their best to obstruct you, but stick to your resolution. A student says, "All teachers are my enemies." He says this because that's the belief stuck in his mind. This belief causes such situations to manifest in which he gets into trouble with his teachers. So, what should he do in this scenario? Without supporting the negative emotions against his teachers, he must instead change his thought to: "All enemies are my teachers." This will change his feeling, his attitude, and eventually his situation. In fact, we must all support the thought that everyone teaches us something.

Emotions will continue to rise; do not get attached to them at once, do not get carried away by them, do not feel miserable believing them to be true… wait and take a pause… see what's coming next.

Due to lack of patience, we blindly believe any event to be true without knowing the truth behind it, and end up reacting to it. We forget that this is not *the end*. There could be a better time coming. The present situation is God's Will Part I. The future will bring in something else. Everything will take place as per the divine plan of God, and there can be nothing better for us than God's divine plan. When we have this faith, we will wait patiently and then get to see astounding results.

You may believe your current life situation is the truth of your life which won't change, but no one knows what is hidden in the future. You may continue to feel hopeless without knowing what is in store for you in the time to come. The moment something doesn't happen as desired, you start feeling disheartened. Instead, tell yourself, "Watch and wait with wonder… Let me wait a bit and see what happens, with the feeling of wonder." Give a pause to your thoughts and emotions. Wait and see what will take place in the coming time. You will witness unexpected and unprecedented outcomes.

We tend to suppress the emotions that we cannot express. These suppressed emotions are harmful for our body. In the beginning, the body endures everything and we do not pay any attention to it. But everything has its limits. Gradually, the body begins to show the negative effects. The weaker organs of the body weaken further and eventually fall prey to a disease.

On the other hand, some people commit the most heinous crimes under the influence of emotions. They may even kill someone because they have never been trained to develop emotional maturity. This subject should in fact be included in the school curriculum. Children should be taught to understand emotions and how to deal with them. This is also essential for maintaining good health, otherwise the body falls sick due to emotional imbalance. And it is important to learn not just about our own emotions but also that of others, in order to behave in the right manner with them.

Learning how to be emotionally mature

Getting rid of physical weakness as well as mental weakness is in our hands. The main cause of mental weakness is emotional immaturity, which means we are a slave to our emotions instead of being their master. To be emotionally strong, we must learn to face our emotions in the right manner. Emotions have been playing with us till date; it's now time to play with our emotions. How? Let's understand this with the help of a story.

> There was a boy called Raghu who would sell flowers outside a temple. He had been feeling discouraged because he wasn't getting many customers. One day, he decided to approach his spiritual master with this problem. The master heard him and said, "Consider selling flowers not as work but as play. Right from young kids to elders, everyone in today's world loves to play computer games. You too should work as if you are playing a computer game."
>
> As per instructions, today Raghu was supposed to try this new experiment of converting his work into play. Hence, he replaced his old slogan of shouting, "Come and buy flowers," to a new one: "Come and buy the enchanting scents of exquisite flowers." People who heard him felt curious and purchased his flowers. The next day Raghu again came up with a new slogan: "Loveliest bouquets at the lowest price." Customers were once again drawn to his stall. Using a fresh slogan every day, he would regard his work as a game. Whether anyone bought flowers from him or not, he wouldn't feel disheartened and instead continue to play with enthusiasm.

This story is symbolic. The stall symbolizes our body, customers represent our emotions, and Raghu means us—the one who watches and listens to customers, i.e., emotions. Just like emotions, there are all kinds of customers. Some customers are about to walk in but leave abruptly, while others come in but don't purchase any flowers.

Some pay attention, while others stop paying attention after some time. But now Raghu has changed his ways of work and learned to handle his customers in the right way. This means he has changed his perspective towards his emotions and learned how to deal with them in the appropriate manner.

Earlier, when his sales were down, he was worried and stressed. This would often cause him to fall sick. Now, since his sales were up, he was happy.

> Due to his interesting attitude and playfulness, his customers began to increase by the day. In a short time, his clientele grew so much that he could not handle them. Seeing this situation, some customers took advantage and stole flowers or even money from his cash box. Sometimes, they would also lie saying that they had given him a hundred rupee note, when they hadn't. Thus, customers (emotions) began to fool him, just like the boy who fooled a shopkeeper in the following way.
>
> > *A boy went to a shop and purchased items worth Rs 45. He gave a 5 rupee note to the shopkeeper. He had drawn a zero just after the number 5 on this note. He handed it to the shopkeeper and said, "Take this 50 rupee note." The man looked at it and smiled. "Oh! So, you think you are very smart!" He took a 50 rupee note from his cash box, cut the zero on it, and slapped it into the boy's palm, saying, "Take these 5 rupees."*

This shows how foolish the shopkeeper could be! Raghu too was becoming an emotional fool by getting trapped in the web of emotions. Although his clientele had increased, his profits had reduced. He was once again falling prey to stress and illness.

When his difficulties became too much, he once again consulted his master, who gave him a solution. "Appoint three employees for yourself: Wisdom, Equanimity, and Awareness."

If you wish to learn how to handle emotions effectively, you must always be equipped with the above three qualities.

With wisdom, you are able to distinguish between real and pseudo emotions, and prevent yourself from supporting pseudo emotions.

Equanimity reminds you to watch all emotions with equanimity. To master your emotions, it teaches you to watch both joy and sorrow with the same attitude.

Awareness will introduce you to the art of watching all emotions with alertness. It prevents you from being consumed by emotions.

Raghu takes the help of these three employees to avoid falling prey to customers (emotions) that appear at his stall (body). Now whenever emotions assail him, all three begin to alert him. "Sir, you must watch everything calmly. Watch your breath too. As soon as the rate of breathing normalizes, you must begin to work; or rather play. Look at emotions as if watching a movie. Just as the movie has no impact on the screen, similarly there should be no impact of emotions on you."

As mentioned earlier, people often hold their breath while listening to some bad news. This causes the emotion to get implanted within the mind and form emotional knots in the future. These knots become the cause of suffering. Hence, you must remain normal and calm in all situations of life. Also, breathe normally while listening to any negative news.

Another important point Raghu's master emphasized is that every customer is supposed to pay him and increase his wealth, and not steal or take from him.

This means that whenever you watch any emotion, you must ensure that each emotion gives you something in return and enhances your wealth of happiness instead of robbing you. When you are able to do that, your level of happiness will increase.

Thus, you can say that you have learnt to watch, understand, and deal with emotions in the right manner when emotions do not make you suffer, or cause you worry and stress, or make a fool out of you. Your breathing will then be normal in all situations. This means no emotion will be able to obstruct your breath.

In this way, with the help of wisdom, equanimity, and awareness, a divine song will pour out from your being: *"Love, Bliss, and Stillness."* Every cell of your body will echo with: *"What's within everyone? Love, bliss, and stillness."* Your every interaction will reflect these three divine attributes and you will be expressing them every moment. Whichever emotion may appear, your body and mind will chant, *"Love, bliss, stillness."*

However, merely uttering these words is completely different from love, bliss, and stillness flowing naturally from within you. These will flow only when you start understanding emotions. You will encounter emotions everywhere, outside your home and within your home. On arrival of each emotion, all you must say is, "Love, bliss, stillness." Whether the road is bumpy or someone says something unpleasant, simply recite, "Love, bliss, stillness."

Thus, in every situation, use wisdom, equanimity, and awareness. Consider every emotion as a play and perform your work as if you are playing a game. This will solve all your problems and fill your heart with love, bliss, and stillness.

Looking at emotions like a game

It's not just emotions that come in various forms. People too are varied in nature and each one has different experiences. That is why, each person reacts differently to a given situation. Emotional reaction to any event is the result of emotional knots or previous experiences of an individual; so how can they be the same as anyone else?

For example, when a customer arrives at the flower stall and says, "I am the temple priest. I've come to request some donation for the temple." Raghu gives him some donation. This is in contradiction to his master's instruction, because when emotions arrive, they are supposed to pay you and not make you pay. They are supposed to help Raghu enhance his wealth and make him emotionally mature. These emotions are like swindlers. You must not get trapped or be ruled by them. Neither should you regard them as the truth and support them.

You must deal with every emotion differently as each emotion is different, has a different impact, and a different location in the body. Just like every customer is different and needs different flowers. Offer a lotus to the one who looks dirty and a sunflower to the one who looks dull and devoid of any sparkle in the eye. Offer jasmine oil to the one who has messed up hair and a rose to the one who looks happy. These flowers represent different emotions, which must be gratified as per their need. When these emotions are satisfied, only then they will surrender and not accumulate within you. They will simply come and go. That's not all; the next time you encounter them, you will be less troubled by them. Otherwise, these emotions will trouble you a lot and will only cause more suffering and stress as you age. On the other hand, if you learn the art of dealing with emotions, the song that will be reverberating in your body-mind will be "Love, joy, stillness," which will endow you with a priceless treasure.

Every jolt that life gives you causes pain but also imparts a lesson. This lesson is like a priceless gem.

The conclusion is that we should learn how the assault of emotions won't be able to hurt us and instead make us emotionally mature. Every emotion arises to fade off. They are impermanent, temporary, and transient. Hence, watch every emotion like a game and don't let them turn into emotional knots.

In the following chapters, we will learn 8 methods of dealing with emotions and releasing negative emotions. This will help us to achieve emotional freedom and discover our true self.

SHARE WITH THE RIGHT PERSON

When an emotion is confronted openly, only then it weakens and breaks down. Else, it strengthens and eats away at your body, making it hollow from within.

There are people who express their emotions openly when drunk, and easily speak out the wrong deeds they have committed, the people they have troubled, and so forth. When they openly talk about it and accept their mistakes, they feel lighter. The liquor aids them in expressing all that was suppressed in their minds. As long as emotions are suppressed within, they are strong and continue to trouble. They lose their strength and become weak as soon as they are expressed. But the drunk individual is under the wrong impression that liquor helped him feel better. However, we know that drinking and expressing our emotions cannot be the right way to release them.

The better way is to open your heart and share your emotions with the right person. The right person could be your sibling or friend or your parent or a counselor or church priest. If you have committed a mistake or a sin, accept it in front of a reliable person and repent it. Your negative emotions are released on repenting and you start feeling lighter. Otherwise, people keep these emotions within due to shame and keep suffering, which then leads to illnesses.

Therefore, search for the right person. The right person is the one with whom you can express your emotions freely and get rid of the burden that was weighing you down. Emotions lose their power once you express them. That is why, you must now find an individual before whom you do not feel ashamed or guilty. Shame corrodes the body and mind. But shame holds power only until it is kept hidden. As soon as it is expressed, it loses all its power over you.

Now the question is, whom should you select as the right person? The right person should be one who keeps your confessions to himself/herself and does not misuse it. One who is your true well-wisher. One who gives you the right advice after scrutinizing and taking everything into consideration. If there is no such person available for you, write down what is in your mind, your suppressed emotions, your guilt, your anger, everything, on a paper and burn it. This is just like one who screams from the top of a hill to vent one's frustration, or one who shouts out his anger at the picture of his boss or mother-in-law or whoever. The person finds relief since the emotions that were agitating him are released.

The method of releasing emotions by sharing with the right person is good but it cannot be a permanent solution. This is because many people take disadvantage of this method. They call up their confidant so many times, that even that individual gets fed up. These outer methods work in the beginning but later it is realized that these are having adverse effects. This is because one becomes dependent on them. Let's understand this with an example.

The person with whom you were sharing your emotions was listening to you intently till yesterday. But today he is not, because he has his own emotions to deal with. You had been venting all your emotions before him but today he himself is boiling with emotions; he is in pain too. When such a situation arrives, you realize that you have become dependent on this method. You are neither able to help yourself nor help him. Hence, it is important that each one of us should learn of permanent and highest ways of releasing emotions.

One such way is to consider your emotions as paying guests. We will learn about it in the next method.

CONSIDER EMOTIONS AS PAYING GUESTS

The second way to gain freedom from emotions is to consider them as your paying guests. Let's understand this method.

As you grow, you sometimes find emotions of fear arising within you, at other times of greed or lust, or a variety of other emotions. Whenever you experience any emotion, check where do you actually feel it within your body. For example, when you feel happy, the happiness is visible on your face but it arises from the heart. The face is merely the outlet of happiness. So, this emotion can be seen on the face but is felt in the heart. Similarly, when the emotion of sorrow or depression arises, it can be felt in the region below the heart and above your navel.

What needs to be done is that whenever an emotion arises, don't be afraid. Just check where you can feel it in the body and then take your attention away from that place. You can do this. Shift your focus from the emotion to your spiritual center, which is roughly the area in the center of your chest. Focus on that sacred space within you.

When you separate yourself from the emotion for some time, its power begins to dissipate. If you are unable to separate, the emotion receives power from you and becomes strong. Its battery is charged up. Hence, you must be able to remove its battery for some time. You can easily accomplish this by learning the art of shifting your focus and witnessing emotions as separate from you.

Consider all the emotions arising in your body as your paying guests. You know that paying guests stay for some time and then leave. When you regard your emotions as paying guests, they will slowly lose their strength and fade away.

There may be some emotions that will stay longer and take more time to fade. Don't worry though, because they will go away too, since they are paying guests.

One more important aspect is that paying guests pay you the rent; you do not pay them. However, we do just the opposite and end up paying the paying guests (the emotions). By focusing on our emotions, we create suffering for ourselves. We consider them to be permanent and feel utter despair. If you suffer and feel despair, it means you paid the rent to the paying guest.

On the other hand, collecting rent from emotions means you learn something from them when they leave. If you are learning to handle emotions, if your mind is becoming steady, pure, loving, and obedient, it means that emotions are paying you the rent. If you are able to see yourself as separate from emotions as well as from the body-mind, it means they are paying you. If you are becoming ready to achieve the ultimate purpose of your life, it means they are paying you.

However, if you are not learning anything from them and only suffering because of them, it means you are paying them. That's not smart. It implies that a paying guest not only stays at your house but also collects rent from you while leaving! Therefore, you need to remind yourself, "*I* am supposed to collect the rent." That is why, it is important that you should not be afraid of any emotion that appears. Tell yourself, "This is a paying guest and will be leaving very soon. But until it's here, I must simply observe it and focus on my spiritual center."

Remind yourself again if you ever forget this crucial point. It is essential that along with mindfulness, there is remembering and re-remembering as well. That's it. Watch all emotions playfully and with ease. This will remove their battery and they will dissolve. They stay for a longer duration only when you charge their battery by getting attached to them, focusing on them, and suffering due to them.

Continue to watch your emotions every day as paying guests. You will gradually find yourself becoming an expert in this art. Emotions and thoughts will then become your slaves. If you practice this regularly, the pain caused by negative thoughts and emotions will slowly cease.

As you grow, various emotions appear in the body, but they all come to teach you something. Some people consider emotions as their enemies and keep fighting them. If you fight with emotions like greed, lust, hatred, or fear, they will only become more powerful. You must affirm, "I am God's property; no negative emotion can trouble me." This will help you to keep your focus on the positive side, on your center, on the understanding that you have gained, and on learning. With this, the power of negative emotions will cease to exist.

ASK YOURSELF THE RIGHT QUESTION

There is often a storm of emotions and sensations raging inside an individual. Every event and every interaction leaves some good or bad feelings inside us. Harsh words or criticism leave a heaviness in the chest. Fear causes pressure in the stomach. The burden of responsibilities shows its effects on the shoulders and back. Altogether, it does not feel good. To get rid of this bad feeling, the mind tends to blame someone or keeps grumbling. This provides relief for at least some time. It does not know of any other way to discharge the disagreeable emotions.

There is in fact a good way to do that. Whenever a negative emotion arises within you, immediately ask yourself: ***"Is this an illusion, a fact, the truth, or the divine truth?"***

The right question has great power. People who ask the right questions are the ones who make great progress in life. That's not all; they are also able to attain freedom from a miserable life.

What is illusion, fact, truth, or the divine truth?

Let's understand the meaning of these four distinct entities. 'Illusion' means something appears to be real but actually isn't. For example, if you insert a straight, long, and thin stick into the water, the stick appears to be crooked but it isn't. In the dark, a coat hanging on a hook can look like a ghost. However, these are merely illusions.

Coming to 'fact', there can be a lot of logic and experience to prove a fact, yet it is not necessary that every fact is the truth. Those who have never studied science will never know or believe while walking on the ground that the Earth is round. They will have their logic and experience that the Earth is straight and flat and they are standing straight on it. Even on the Equator or in the Southern Hemisphere, people feel the same, since this is what they see and feel. But we know the 'truth'. The truth is that a person who is hanging upside down or standing crooked on Earth believes himself to be standing straight because of the gravitational force of Earth.

Similarly, there is the illusion of sunset due to the Earth's rotation. Sometimes it is felt that the sun has set when it is shrouded by clouds. At night, it becomes a fact that the sun has set. Although, the truth is the sun neither rises nor sets; it remains the same. Our location changes as the Earth rotates, due to which we cannot see the sun at night. The shape of the moon too looks different on different days; that's a fact. Sometimes it appears to be full and at other times half or crescent, but the truth is it remains the same, neither waxing nor waning.

However, the biggest illusion that man harbors is that he dies when his body expires. It is also a fact for him since "dead" people are no longer visible after the body is destroyed. But the truth is that the journey of their life continues further in the astral form.

Above and beyond the illusion, fact, and truth, is the 'divine truth'. The divine truth is that there is no such thing as birth and death. There is just one Consciousness that is manifesting in various forms to play this divine game or *leela*. It is not born and it does not die. It just *is*. It is the only truth and everything else is an illusion created by it. Various forms, various bodies, as well as their birth and death is an illusion, even if it appears real.

Thus, whenever distressing emotions arise due to some thought, ask yourself right away, "Is this thought an illusion, a fact, the truth, or the divine truth? Is this thought my misbelief? Can a single thought have so much power to cause me suffering? What are the facts related to this thought? Is this thought the truth or the divine truth?" In this way, several such questions will assist you in bringing the reality to light. Like, "What is sorrow, why does it occur, from where does it appear, and why do we keep feeling miserable?"

If the smallest of things is making us unhappy, it definitely means we are harboring some misbeliefs, illusions, ignorance, unconsciousness, or something else that causes us pain. To find a solution, we will have to ask ourselves the above questions, and learn the art of conversing with ourselves.

Suppose, someone says something bad to you, you feel hurt and declare right away: "People are bad." In this situation, ask yourself the question, "Is this my delusion, or a fact, or the truth, or the divine truth?"

(You should be aware that the thought "people are bad" can attract bad people in your life, as almost everything in your life manifests as per your thoughts.)

So, then, is it your delusion that people are bad or is it a fact? It is a fact because people have behaved wrongly with you. You may have a lot of evidence to prove your statement, since you have seen their wrong behavior many times. So, it is a fact. (Although you know that not all people are bad, nor are the "bad" people bad with everyone.)

Now the question is, is it the truth? It may be a fact that people behave badly but the truth is that people are not bad but are helpless due to their tendencies. Their compulsive tendencies force them to be and to do bad. Whatever bad spouts from them is because of their helplessness. This happens because they want to release and be free from their agitating emotions, but do not know the right way to do so.

For example, your boss urgently needs to use the bathroom, but all the bathrooms are occupied. You know how it feels in that condition. He comes out in your cubicle and starts yelling, "Why can't you make proper arrangements… why nobody bothers about such things… how many times have I said what should be done, but does anybody listen?!" You have no idea why he is lashing at you, and you conclude, "People are bad." If you knew that his helplessness is making him behave in this manner, you would not have arrived at that conclusion. In fact, you would have probably thought of how to help him out.

This was just an example, but people do have various tendencies and painful emotions that are boiling within them and tormenting them. They *need* to release these emotions and therefore burst out. Because we are unaware of this, we feel hurt and think they are bad.

The fourth aspect of the question is: "Is it the divine truth that people are bad?" The divine truth is that every individual is the manifest form of the formless, divine Consciousness. So, how can anyone be bad? It is Consciousness that is playing a negative role through some bodies and positive through others—since there is nothing else besides Consciousness. This is its divine game going on since eternity. So, there is no question of someone being bad or good.

Therefore, "people are bad" is an illusion, but it is a fact for you, although it is neither the truth nor the divine truth. When we have this knowledge and remember it, then we won't feel hurt when someone says something bitter to us.

Let us consider one more example. Suppose, you are sometimes plagued with thoughts such as: "What if I become poor… hope someone hasn't stolen money from my account… what if the bankers make some mistake… there are so many frauds taking place these days…" These thoughts cause tremendous worry and anxiety. The first thing to do is to calm down. Then ask yourself the correct question: "Is this my delusion, a fact, the truth, or the divine truth? I must go and find the truth. A solution cannot be found if I simply continue to worry. And henceforth, I will also be careful while spending money." In this way, you can avoid the unnecessary stress caused by negative thoughts. Your contemplation will begin as soon as you ask the right questions. You may start thinking, "Maybe what I'm pondering is just a delusion. I will check with the bank first."

There are people in the world who travel without money. And if they do get money, they buy a ticket for the last stop of the train they are boarding. This is because they know that they need to disembark there and further travel would get arranged as and when they arrive there. They just go with the flow. Are these people poor? We normally consider those people as poor who never had any money. In fact, they never had money till the end of their lives, yet lived happily. So, were they poor? Or are those people poor who had a lot of money, yet remained unhappy throughout their lives? If you have the right understanding, you would agree that the second type of people are poor. They had money to do anything and always traveled by first class, yet they were poor, because they were always fearful about the plane getting hijacked or exploding in mid-air. Another fear was, "I have money today. What if I don't have it tomorrow? What if it all gets stolen?" They lived their entire lives in fear. This is poverty.

By contemplating in this manner, the thoughts of losing money that were troubling you will disperse along with the fear and anxiety.

Your negative or positive reaction to a person, event, or thought, is a seed of karma, which is at the level of emotions. This seed of karma yields the corresponding fruit. Hence, it is very important to understand emotions. If you can understand them, only then you can ask the right question as soon as they arise, and come out of them. Positive emotions will bring positive results. Thus, you are able to live a happy life when you gain the knowledge that helps you to be free from negative tendencies, thoughts, and emotions.

USE THIS POWERFUL MANTRA

Man leads a double life when he deceives and cheats people due to greed. One life is that which he displays for others, and the other which he actually lives. He has to strive a lot all his life to maintain this farce. As a result, he lives in constant physical and psychological stress. For example, there are people who are not wealthy, but keep borrowing and taking loans, simply to show the world that they are living a grand life. Eventually, when their truth comes out, they are at the edge of bankruptcy and about to lose even their house. An individual who leads a life of deceit causes harm not just to oneself, but knowingly or unknowingly inspires others to commit deceit too.

The lies that we tell ourselves are much more dangerous than the ones we tell others. This is because we rarely realize when we lie to ourselves. It is easier to catch the lies that we tell others and therefore relatively easier to avoid. Whereas the lies we tell ourselves or the wrong notions that we believe in are difficult to catch and avoid. Such lies affect our emotional well-being and we begin to feel uncomfortable.

There is a little question that can help you to avoid lying to yourself. In fact, it is not just a question but a powerful mantra. All you need to do is answer this question truthfully. Henceforth, whenever an emotion overwhelms you or your mind cannot stop grumbling and making excuses, ask yourself: **"Whatever I have received, how much does it weigh?"**

This question may seem strange, so let's see what it means.

Think of all the things that you get in life. You get joy and suffering, positive and negative feelings, good and bad scenes to watch, good and bad words to listen, appreciation, criticism, and so on. You are constantly getting something all your life. So, whatever you are getting, how much does it weigh? This means, how much is its worth or importance, or how much does it really hurt?

Answer this question honestly, without amplifying or hiding anything. For example, you are working and your mind says, "Oh God! I am feeling so tired." Ask yourself, "How much does this tiredness weigh? How much am I really tired? Am I actually very tired or just a little? And exactly what is tired—the back, the legs, or the brain? It can be that the fatigue is just a little bit but there is more of laziness or lethargy. Maybe only a few parts of the body are exhausted, but I am proclaiming that I am very tired." So, you must tell yourself the whole truth because an honest person always stays happy and at peace.

Let's take another example. Suppose, you saw a scene that disturbed you or watched some news that upset you. Ask yourself, "How much does this scene or this news weigh? It may seem heavy to me, but it could be weighing just 5-10 grams. Could it be that my thoughts are making it heavier?" In this way, tell the truth to yourself.

Some people tend to get more affected by words. For instance, they keep on ruminating, "My neighbor said *this* to me, my wife spoke like *this*, my husband uttered *such* words, my boss used wrong language with me..." Many a time, we feel so bad about certain words, that we are stuck to them all our lives. In such cases, ask yourself, "Whatever I received in those scenarios, how much does it weigh? How much do those words weigh?" The truth will unfold and you will realize that the issues were not that huge. Our wrong focus, our thoughts, and ego were making them seem bigger.

If you are feeling unhappy, it means there is a negative emotion in the body. Check how much does it weigh (i.e. how much is it hurting)? Check where do you feel it in your body. In the chest, above the navel, or in your forehead? Where do you feel it exactly? If you tell the truth to yourself, you will know that it is not much and also it is not permanent. As you investigate the negative emotion in this manner, you will find that in the process it has already vanished.

Not just the negative emotions but watching also the positive ones like pleasure, praise, credit, etc. in this manner will break your unconsciousness. Your attachment to those emotions will cease and they will no longer be able to trap you. Suppose, someone lavishes fake or exaggerated praises upon you. "Wowww! Just look at you... you're looking awesome... there is no one as fabulous as you in the entire party." Now you are lost in those thoughts the whole day. Investigate these pleasant feelings too with awareness and consider them candidly. This will enable you to clearly observe your rising ego as well as save you from the wrong intentions of that person, if any.

Using the mantra "How much does it weigh?" for every event throughout the day will raise your awareness. The habit of overstating or understating things will break. Otherwise, we tend to look at our emotions in a magnified manner and increase their impact. It is especially damaging in case of negative emotions; we suffer even that which we haven't received. On the other hand, looking at our goodness or greatness in an exaggerated manner inflates our ego. To prevent both situations, we must honestly ask ourselves in every event, "How much does it weigh?"

PRACTICE MEDITATION

Let's assume that it's dark and you are alone in a jungle, which is home to all kinds of animals. You can hear the frightening sounds of their approaching movement and their growls and calls. You find it hard to breathe with terror coursing through your body. Suddenly, lightning strikes, and in that light you see that although the forest is all around you, but you are standing within a huge glass dome. You are totally secure. That's it. As soon as you see this, your panic disappears because now you are convinced that no creature can reach you. Although a moment back, you had heard snakes hissing and scorpions crawling towards you, as well as the roar of lions and tigers, but now you are totally free from fear.

This is the fifth way to achieve freedom from negative emotions, which you can adopt in your daily life. To learn it you need to listen to discourses and read books that impart the supreme truth, as well as practice meditation.

Exactly what are you supposed to do in this meditation? **You have to face your emotions and feel them fully.** Experience all your emotions completely. Don't be afraid of being hurt by them (like from the wild animals) because emotions are occuring in your body-mind, not in the real you. They cannot touch the real you.

Begin with experiencing the smaller emotions completely, and then with the right understanding, experience the emotions that arise from bigger incidents in your life. When you begin to experience your emotions fully, you start becoming free from them. After that, there remains no place for failure in your life. Otherwise, one tends to get depressed due to failure, which in turn causes failure once again. One's entire life can be spent in this vicious cycle of failure and depression.

To avoid this cycle, all you need to do is experience each emotion fully. Continue to do this until the emotions start dissolving, because only after that you will be totally free of those emotions. Also ensure that no emotion gets the chance of solidifying and settling inside your mind.

You have to practice meditation so that you can release emotions easily. People all over the world are releasing their emotions—emotions that they have suppressed within them. Some are releasing anger, some are releasing love, while some are releasing lust. The good thing about meditation is that it helps to release all kinds of emotions with ease and harmony, which causes no harm to anyone.

Watch yourself and check which emotion has arisen within you. Whichever emotion arises any time, release it. People who do not practice meditation are unable to let go of their emotions easily. They then search for external ways to release them and get tangled in thoughts such as, "What should I do… how can I convey that which I am unable to speak out... whom should I tell this...." Such thoughts only give rise to further complications.

With meditation, such thoughts will end and you will be able to discharge your emotions in a better manner. So, let us learn how to practice this meditation.

Face and Feel Fully Meditation

It's best to first read the entire meditation given below and understand the technique. Then you can proceed to practice this meditation.

1. Close your eyes. Like a spectator, watch with detachment which emotion is present in which part of your body—above your stomach, on the side, in the chest, on the back, or elsewhere.

2. Whatever the situation, watch it only as an observer. Do not keep any attachment to any emotion.

3. Practice this meditation in silence every day. Only then will you be able to learn and master it.

4. Wherever you experience the emotions on your body, focus there, and check how it feels—heavy or light, pleasant or unpleasant, joyful or fearful, worrisome or anxious. Simply experience these emotions, without labeling them as good or bad.

5. Go through your whole body, part by part. During this inner journey, you will realize that no emotion is permanent, it is in fact temporary. If it's there one moment, the next moment it's not. If it's there today, tomorrow it's not. Just observe like a silent spectator.

6. Without being affected by events taking place outside or within, experience the emotions. Then slowly open your eyes. Remain in this state for some time and then proceed with your usual activities.

By practicing this meditation, you learn to come out of your emotions. You get closer to your true self. As soon as you reach close to your true divine self, the emotions begin to dissolve. You feel free.

With consistent practice of meditation, you actually realize and experience that you are the formless, divine self, and all the emotions that were threatening to overwhelm you in the jungle of life, simply cannot touch you. You are separate from the emotions. You are safe. You are always safe.

Thus, whenever you feel unhappy, you should know that nature is indicating: "You have moved away from your true self. Go back to your self." As soon as you return to your true divine self, happiness begins to flow. Then everything that you desire starts coming to you effortlessly with the free flow of life.

Freedom from Childhood Emotions with Releasing Meditation

Whenever the painful emotions of your childhood rear their heads, you must through reflection and meditation remind yourself, "If I am still carrying the fears and sorrows of my past, then I got to let them go."

In order to release the suppressed emotions of negative incidents of your childhood, take out some time every day and practice the *Releasing Meditation*.

1. Sit in a comfortable posture with eyes closed. Close your fists.

2. Whichever emotions arise, or that which are accumulated or suppressed within, release them all by slowly opening your fists and saying, "Let go… let go… let go."

    During this process, harbor the understanding that it is nobody's fault. With the feeling of gratitude, tell your suppressed emotions, "Thank you for freeing yourself and me."

3. Say, "Let go… let go…" aloud as well as within your mind. You can also lift your hands up and say it with all your heart.

    This is how whatever is accumulated within you will be released. Stop supporting untrue emotions. Whenever any emotion appears, do not consider it to be the truth. Learn to watch it without backing it or criticizing it.

4. In the end, bring your childhood events before your eyes and raise both your hands towards the skies and say, "I am releasing all these negative incidents into the universe… I am releasing them forever… I am free from them, I am free, I am free, I am freedom."

5. Remain in this state for some time and then slowly open your eyes. You can then resume your routine activities.

Until you attain liberation from all negative incidents, fears, and sorrows, practice this meditation regularly. In this way, with understanding, let go of all that has collected within you. Whatever you have gathered in ignorance, the stories you have created in your mind regarding people and events, all of these want to be set free forever. Everything suppressed within you desperately wishes to come out and leave, due to which your body may experience some discomfort. Don't be afraid, as it will last only for some time. Thereafter, you will notice the difference in your feeling. What you were feeling till yesterday, you will no longer be feeling today. This is because some things are being released. Let this process continue regularly.

During this process, do not entertain thoughts like, "How long is this going to take… how will this happen, there is so much accumulated inside… is it possible to be totally free or not…" Instead, continue this practice religiously along with all your regular activities. Thus, your normal life and your inner cleansing will go on hand in hand. This is a beautiful way of discharging your suppressed emotions.

Every person who wishes to stay happy, must learn the art of feeling fully as well as releasing emotions with the help of meditation, and master it with consistent practice. You automatically get several opportunities throughout the day. The one who truly understands this, derives benefit from every opportunity that comes their way.

WITNESS EMOTIONS WITH DETACHMENT

From your childhood to your present, various events gave rise to various emotions, which are buried deep within you. Some positive or negative emotions emerge in the body in every incident and with every interaction that you have with anyone. Since we do not like the negative emotions, we try to avoid them by escaping them. Because we have been running away from these emotions for many years, they have got buried deep within us. This happens because we were not aware of how to deal with them.

We are now learning the art of dealing with our emotions and we now understand that if any emotion appears, instead of escaping it, we must watch it simply as a detached witness or spectator. When we run away from an emotion, it tends to gradually get stronger. But when we accept it and witness it, it loses its strength. Whenever a negative or painful emotion crops up, instead of avoiding it, observe it as separate from you, with the understanding, "This emotion is transient in nature; it does not last long. Let me see how long it stays."

Actually, your body communicates with you through emotions and hence it is essential to learn to witness them, whether you like them or not.

For example, when a kid in the family draws something on a piece of paper, he insists you take a look at it. You say, "Not now, I am busy. I'll see it later." After some time, you take a look at the picture. Most often, we do not like those pictures, because the child is immature and his drawing is made up of some crooked lines. However, the child feels it is beautiful. Therefore, even if you don't like the drawing, you take a close look at it and exclaim, "What a beautiful picture!"

We must watch the emotions that arise in our body in the same way. Watch them as they are, without labeling them as good or bad. It is natural for different emotions to emerge in different situations. As soon as you witness an emotion, with detachment, it will cease to trouble you. You must master this art, so that there remains no reason for them to get suppressed in your mind. You can then stay happy by achieving freedom from negative emotions in this manner.

Watch the tension created by thoughts as a witness

Negative thoughts generally trigger misery and guilt. Therefore, whenever such thoughts occur, ask yourself, "Where are these thoughts arising within my body?" Check where do you feel their tension or disagreeable feeling—on the navel, below the chest, on the shoulders, or in your eyes. Once you locate it, do not escape it nor prolong it; only witness it.

Actually these are thoughts that were suppressed and are now trying to surface; they will fade away once you witness them. This is the art. Generally, people try to escape from such thoughts. As soon as these thoughts arise, they try to distract themselves by watching television, or reading the newspaper, or drinking, or something else. This only serves to intensify those thoughts. Hence, do not try to run away from them, just witness them.

In fact, instead of running away from them, you can make them a medium for your progress. However, this is not possible until you have clarity that you can do this. Detached witnessing will help you gain this clarity.

If the intensity of a thought is too much and you are unable to watch it as a witness, then say to yourself, "I am enclosing it in a box and releasing it into the universe." This means you should give that thought a shape, color, and some distinct identity. Then visualize yourself placing it into a box and releasing it into the universe. You will be surprised after doing this because you will find that the tension created by that thought has ceased as well as you are free from that thought.

Until you learn the art of witnessing your thoughts the right way and thus converting snakes into ladders, continue to practice the various methods given in this book. Remember that you must not fight with any of your thought or oppose it saying, "Why did this happen? It shouldn't have happened with me…" and so on. If a thought and the emotion created by it exists, then it exists. It can be dissolved by simply watching it.

Watch your problems as a witness

When our mind repeatedly opposes the thoughts arising from problems, then those thoughts take root in the mind instead of going away. Hence, whenever such thoughts appear, first accept them and allow them. Then check where in the body do you feel the emotions or sensations triggered by those thoughts. There may be heaviness, pressure, constriction, or a negative feeling in specific parts of the body. Watch these with detachment and without labeling them.

Very often, when we do not wish to see these emotions, they pop up time and again. To dissolve them permanently, witnessing is the method. This is important for everyone. Some emotions or some events are suppressed deep within you, which suddenly crop up at times. They will gradually disperse on witnessing them with detachment. However, many people either suppress them again or vent them by shouting, screaming, getting angry or distressed. They do this in an attempt to find some relief for a while. But the problems only tend to multiply.

To dissolve these problem-related emotions, you must witness them like you would watch a naughty child, without attaching any labels. When you will be successful in doing this, you will notice that their power has significantly reduced the next time they appear. In this way, you will be able to gradually gain freedom from them.

DO NOT CONSIDER YOURSELF AS THE BODY

You are the infinite Self or Consciousness. You forget this supreme truth and consider yourself to be the body. This is the fundamental cause of emotions causing you suffering. What you actually are, is free from the beginning, and no emotion or anything else can touch it. If you can grasp this basic principle, all the emotions and problems will dissolve at once.

Emotions exist only in the body, not in the "real you." Even on the body, they are temporary. You may have seen several emotions rising in the body and fading away every day. If you were to count the emotions that emerged from the first day you were born to the present day, they will number in the millions. This is because they do not stop occurring, they are transient in nature, and they come and go. Understanding this is maturity.

When a child becomes mature, he or she stops collecting colored stones, shells, and other odds and ends in their pockets. Similarly, when you are ready to become emotionally mature, you will say to yourself, "I have to stop getting entangled or swayed by my emotions. If they appear, let them; and if they disappear, let them." This is the right choice.

We always think that if our body experiences pleasant emotions, it will be good for us. Thinking thus, we either try to shoo away unpleasant emotions or escape from them and get ensnared by various addictions in the process. We don't know how to face these emotions. Fighting with emotions or striving to drive them away is as useless as a leopard trying to change its spots. If you have been unwittingly trying to do so, it's time to stop. Let's understand how this can be done through an example.

Suppose you are struggling to find the answer to an impossible puzzle. Someone comes and tells you, "Not searching for the solution is the solution to this puzzle." You will instantly stop your endeavor. It's the same with emotions. The day you realize the futility of fighting emotions, you will stop it. Otherwise, whether you are busy working or waiting in a queue, internally you are wrestling with some emotion or the other. This is not required at all. Trying to find a solution to something that has no solution is a folly.

However, our tendency is to not believe it until we realize it on our own. When we are told that emotions are merely occurring on the body and hence there is no need to wrestle with them or try to find their solution, we are quick to snap, "You have no idea what I'm feeling. Only I know my pain and suffering." But we need to realize the truth and this realization can occur only when we learn the art of detached witnessing. Most importantly, we need to know and understand that the emotions have arisen not within us but on the body. The body is merely a vehicle, a tool, or an instrument, which we are using. Ask yourself, "Even when emotions arise in my vehicle, can it still function as it is supposed to?" The answer will be, "Yes, it can." After that, let your body sit in silence with eyes closed for some time and let it witness the emotion which is troubling it. Make it realize that the emotion which it feels is huge and overpowering is not really that big; it is small. We need to learn this art.

Suppose, during the rainy season someone yelps, "Snake... snake!!!" When you run to see it, you find that it's just a tiny little snake which is seen only during the rains and is not poisonous. You realize that the person was screeching with fear about something that was actually not at all huge or dreadful. When you realize this, you will not give it much importance.

Likewise, you must not give much importance to any emotion. When you recognize that the emotion is actually quite small, you will decide, "I am supposed to complete this project and I'll not halt it just because this emotion has appeared. It's not that big to warrant discontinuation of work. Work can be done and required decisions can be taken in spite of the presence of this emotion."

For instance, if you are supposed to go somewhere or help someone, you can do it even when some emotions are present in your body. No emotion can stop you. This is because it has appeared in the body and not in you. The body will continue its work and you can continue yours. The body will be engaged in its job of dissolving the emotion and you can carry on with your job. If you wish to help the body, then you could take some deep breaths, provide some rest to the body, or make it sit in meditation for some time. Do whatever is possible at that time. When you do this, you will find that none of your activities are disrupted due to any emotion and everything is continuing smoothly. Life is going on as it was.

Emotions appear and disappear but your work is not affected. All you have to do is to let the emotions arrive in their flow and leave in their flow. Neither suppress them nor vent them on someone else. When this becomes clear to you, it will have a huge positive impact on your life.

If you don't do this, then you constantly wish that negative emotions should not appear. Nevertheless, they appear and you struggle and wrestle with them, unnecessarily tormenting yourself. If someday a leopard is able to change its spots or you are able to win over an emotion, it will not be a big miracle. This is because even after that, the leopard will remain a leopard and the emotion will remain an emotion. It will appear again and also disappear. When you reflect on this, you will realize that struggling with emotions is pointless because it makes no difference. You are the same even after the emotion arrives.

Actually, emotions are nature's way of giving feedback to you. Do not find fault or add your own story to it. Imagine you receive a pie and you find some gravel or tiny stones in it. You then add a little mud to it and refrigerate it, to eat it later. Anyone who sees this will be aghast and cry out, "What are you doing?! And why?" You do the same thing when an emotion appears in your body. You add your own story to it and store it, so that you can later take it out and recall everything and suffer once again.

This is totally unnecessary. You simply need to watch it as a detached observer. If you were writing something, continue with it despite the emotion. In fact, your writing may be further enhanced due to the emotion. In a way, it is nature's method of assisting you.

Imagine you are writing a poem in your room and an emotion arrives and says, "You will be fired from your job." You can reply,

"There is this poem on one side and getting fired on the other side. Let's see what emerges by combining these two." You will finish working on the poem and then do what's required for your job.

Whether you are writing or doing anything else, don't stop due to emotions. Because that activity is connected to your expression of happiness.

Utilize your mirror like body

In order to avoid getting entangled and attached to your body, remind yourself that the body is your vehicle or a mirror that helps you to experience and express your true self. Affirm to yourself, "I will make the right use of this body as my mirror." Even if the mirror heats up due to some emotions, it will still show you your image. This is possible because you stand at a distance from the mirror. If anger arises within your body, i.e., your mirror gets hot, it can still show you your image. This means you can still experience your true nature. All you need to remember is, "Even if the body is filled with emotions or thoughts, I must experience my true self."

When you sit in meditation, your body may be filled with thoughts. In this situation, remind yourself, "These thoughts have not appeared in me, rather they are running through this mirror before which I am standing." Your body is the mirror in which thoughts, blood, breath, emotions, are flowing. That which is standing before the mirror (your true self) has no blood, breath, or thought; it is formless and thoughtless. It is simply *being*. From there, everything is being known. The real you is witnessing everything, and knowing itself as separate from everything. Thus, it witnesses itself. This is Self Witnessing. When people do not have complete understanding, they stop at being a witness and are not able to proceed any further;

although the actual purpose is to become a Self witness (experiencing your true nature).

The journey from being a witness to becoming a Self witness is in fact the journey from the head to the heart. Hence, whether the mirror (body) is suffused with anger, vices, or thoughts, it will still remain a mirror. It can show you your image. You only need to remember that you have to experience your true self through this body.

Whenever any event occurs, your body fills up with emotions, and many a time the emotions that have been suppressed within for a long time, pour out. You then become so tangled in them that you suffer throughout your life. But as you gradually start shifting to your true self, the suppressed emotions will begin to release and all the emotional knots will start opening.

On realizing the supreme truth, you are able to develop detachment from the body with the understanding: "Emotions, thoughts, or anything else may appear in the body-mind or not, it does not affect my true self." It is only then that you get rid of the wrong belief that you have achieved liberation when emotions do not arise or you don't get influenced by them.

During different seasons, different factors get activated within the body, which give rise to certain emotions. There is no need to achieve freedom from them, since they will continue to appear according to nature's cycle. However, because the mind desires to be free from them, it resists them every time. We must abandon this desire. On the other hand, the emotions arising from wrong beliefs such as hatred or jealousy appear because we think, "Everyone is getting everything, whereas I am not. Maybe those people are different from me." Liberation means freedom from such beliefs.

Depending on the constitution and disposition of your body, whether it belongs to the category of *vata, pitta,* or *kapha,* various things will continue to occur in the body. You must only be free from the desire to resist them. Your understanding should be, "Whether this happens or not, it does not matter." This is liberation in the true sense.

If the definition of liberation was that nothing at all should arise in the body, then liberation was impossible. Here we are talking about liberation which is possible despite anything occurring in the body, which is possible despite negativity or positivity. Until we fully grasp this concept, there can be no liberation. In spite of understanding this, the desire that "this should not happen and that should not happen" will continue to arise again and again, but you must not get ensnared by it.

If you feel, "I got entangled in emotions, I am not capable of achieving liberation," then ignore it. You must hold on to the understanding that you can attain liberation despite all of this. This is the missing link which is the most essential to understand.

FOCUS ON WHAT YOU WANT

When emotions arise in the body, the mind tends to become anxious and restless. Once the emotions subside, the mind returns to its original state. This is what keeps happening in the body that you are using. This occurs due to old memories, moods, seasons, situations, or the environment.

The ocean of emotions that you go through brings about physical and hormonal changes within you, as well as changes in situations and in the behavior of other people. People who were declaring that they will help you, now say they cannot. At such times, you must hold on to the understanding that the trembling you are feeling is normal and natural in the body that you are using for this journey of life. Let us understand this through an example.

Suppose, you have an intense desire to play a harmonium, which is a musical instrument. Someone gives you a harmonium and informs you that sometimes it shudders or vibrates a bit while playing. You say, "No problem. It'll do." This is because all you are interested in is playing the harmonium, listening to the music it creates, practicing with it, and losing yourself in its magic.

You won't tell that person, "I don't want your harmonium if it shudders and vibrates." That's because at that time you can clearly imagine the melodies you will play on it, the songs you will compose, and the divine music that will flow with the combination of the songs and the tunes. You get excited just thinking about it. This harmonium may shudder intermittently like a cell phone on vibration mode, but you think, "With practice, the harmonium may stop vibrating and could stabilize. If it stabilizes, that would be great, but if not, then too it's fine. I can still practice on it."

When you start playing it, you find that it does vibrate sometimes. You would say that you were already informed about this and it does not make any difference to you. But when after many years you forget this, you start thinking, "Why this shuddering and trembling… why do these emotions and feelings of sorrow appear… this should not happen… why is this happening with me?"

To escape that sorrow, one may tend to lean toward an addiction or start venting on people, because this stops the vibration in the harmonium. We then get habituated to this short-cut of venting on others to release our unbearable emotions.

When the vibrations occur, we start yelling even at someone's smallest mistake, because it provides relief. Earlier, we would never shout at anyone upon similar mistakes. Some people get habituated to cursing whoever is present around them. They feel better once they discharge their emotions in this way. They do this because they have never been taught how to get rid of their emotions without hurting themselves and others. People often torture themselves or others when faced with emotions. Those, who do not want to hurt others, have the tendency to suppress their emotions and thereby fall sick.

In this journey of life, if you have this knowledge about emotions, then you can smile even while passing through them. This is because you know that in some time this emotion will scatter away like the clouds, and the sky of your mind will be clear once again. This conviction will be possible because you have seen this happen innumerable times with your emotions. With this, you gain emotional maturity or emotional intelligence. Let's understand this through one more example.

Suppose you have a washing machine which tends to shudder at times. In that case, you don't say, "I am shuddering;" you say that the washing machine is shuddering. Either you continue washing and drying your clothes, or wait awhile. After letting it rest for some time and making some adjustments, you start using it once more to complete your work.

In the above example, the washing machine is symbolic of your body and the one using it is you. When the body shudders, i.e., when emotions crop up on the body, you must be clearly able to see that the shuddering is occurring in the body and not in you.

When you go through life having done this homework, your journey will be smooth because you are aware that occasional trembling will occur in the harmonium or the washing machine, but you are separate from it. When you remain unaffected, people will exclaim, "How come you're not affected?! How is it possible?" You will then be able to say, "I had already done my homework. I knew all of this is going to happen, emotions are going to arise.

Hence, I was fully prepared to watch them as a detached witness, which dissolves them within a short time."

The desire of the mind is that we should not face any suffering or problems. On the contrary, we should think, "Why shouldn't sufferings and problems exist in my life? And if they cease to exist, then what am I planning to do?"

Someone says, "I wish there was no suffering in my life." When asked, "If there is no suffering, what will you do?" he replies, "I will carry out certain activities to serve humanity." He is then told, "Start doing those activities. Your suffering will disappear as a bonus."

If you desire to have lots of money, focus on what you wish to do when you get that money. Do not think, "Since I don't have money, I am unable to do this… there should be no shortage of money in my life."

Instead, think, "What will I do if there is no lack of money? I will carry out this particular work for the betterment of this world." Stay in that emotion of creation. Money will automatically flow toward you; but it's just a bonus. You must be convinced that the things you wish to do are not connected to money. We have erroneously made this connection. If money has a role to play in your life, it will come on its own. But by the end of your life, you will be able to say, "I lived my entire life as I wanted to."

What we learn from this example is that you must focus on the kind of life that you wish to live. Thereby, you will automatically start living that life. Leave all your requirements to nature. Nature will see to it whether or not you need money, a car, or anything else, and provide you accordingly.

Man has linked happiness to money and one's body. Everybody thinks that they will be happy if they have lots of money and a perfect body. There have been so many individuals whose appearance or looks were not liked by others. But once their qualities came to light in front of the world, they were loved by all. Why do we begin to like people of different creeds and races, fair or dark, tall or short, "good-looking" or not? It's because the Self's desire is being fulfilled through those bodies, and hence the Self begins to shine in them. We get a glimpse of the divine self on seeing those individuals and that's why we like them.

We have unconsciously believed that if certain conditions are fulfilled, only then we can do what we want to. However, what you need to do is simply tell nature what you desire. If you are not the body, what would you desire? How would you like to spend your life on Earth? What will happen if emotions did not arise? Focus on the work you would do if emotions ceased to trouble you. Otherwise, we recite all our lives, "There should be no disappointments… no sorrow… no boredom… no anger… no this… no that…" Instead, now imagine what will you create in their absence? Start praying for that. The more the number of people who understand this, the more it will impact everyone on Earth.

You have been releasing your emotions through old ways, now you are aware of new and better ways. This new understanding will show you the right path.

HOW TO USE THE EIGHT METHODS
The Game of Freedom from Emotions

We are often bewildered on encountering dilemmas, difficulties, or hardships. We fail to understand what to do. On the other hand, when a friend or somebody else approaches us with similar problems, we are easily able to advise them. This is because we are not attached to those problems. *This* is the attitude we must adopt for our own difficulties as well.

It may not be possible to share each and every problem with someone else, and therefore we must prepare ourselves for every situation. To do so, we must play a double role—one that of ourselves and the other that of a person who has problems and needs our advice. Let's understand how this can be accomplished.

Suppose you are playing carom or chess, but from both sides. There is no other player. In the same way, you must play from both sides, but in your diary.

Divide the page into two sections: one black and the other white. The left side can be allotted to black and the right to white. On the black side, list your troublesome emotions using a black pen. On the white side, write the methods to deal with each emotion, using any light-colored pen. In this way, you have to play two roles at the same time. While writing your emotions, you are playing yourself. And while writing the solutions, you should assume that you are offering solutions to a friend for his/her negative emotions; assuming that the unpleasant event that has taken place, did not occur with you but with this friend, and you only have to show him the way. You have to do this with detachment; without getting attached to the problem or emotion. This can be called as 'playing chess in your diary.'

You must play this game with complete sincerity. Only then you will gain a new understanding of emotions. By writing in your diary, you will find the way to achieve freedom from negative emotions. Along with this, remember the new alphabet as well. You can use the summary given below from A to I.

A – Share your emotions with an APPROPRIATE PERSON. Watch with AWARENESS where the emotions are located out of the 18 spots in the body.

B – Focus on your BREATH when there is an onslaught of emotions and keep it normal.

C – Consider emotions as a COMPUTER game and deal with them accordingly.

D – DON'T suppress emotions or vent on others. Observe them

as a DETACHED WITNESS.

E – EMOTIONLESS COMMUNICATION. Verbalize your emotions without getting emotional.

F – FACE AND FEEL FULLY Meditation to dissolve emotions and Releasing Meditation to let go of negative emotions. FOCUS on what you want and start doing it.

G – Consider emotions as paying GUESTS and collect rent from them. Remain in the state of GRATITUDE and GRACE.

H – HONESTLY ANSWER: "Is this an illusion, a fact, the truth, or the divine truth?" When feeling hurt by people or events, ask, "HOW MUCH does it weigh?"

I – Look at everything with the understanding: "I am not the body."

Memorize this new alphabet and get ready to be the master of your emotions.

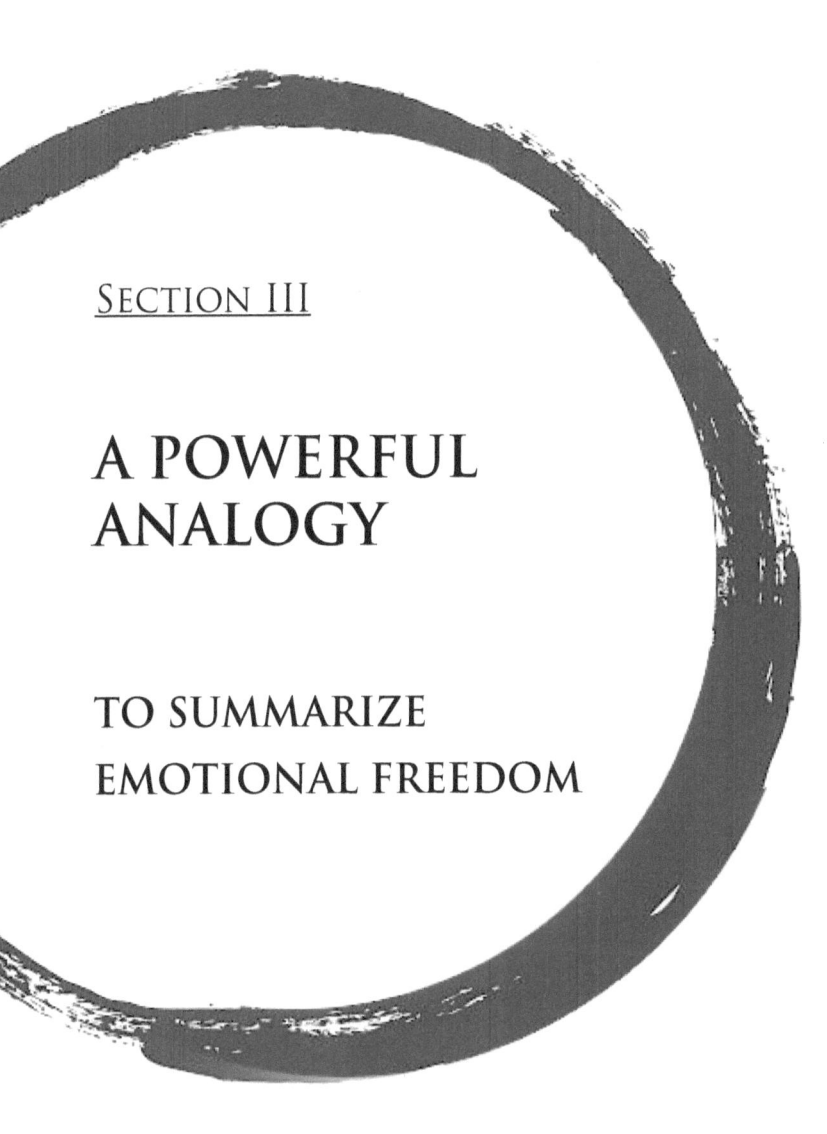

Section III

A POWERFUL ANALOGY

TO SUMMARIZE EMOTIONAL FREEDOM

FIVE-STAR HOTEL

You are the owner of a five-star hotel.

You have happy and satisfied customers.

This is because you never take payment from them;

instead you pay them when they leave.

Do you know about this hotel you own?

.

.

.

It's time to collect the payment.

YOUR FIVE-STAR HOTEL
A Hideout of Negative Emotions

There is a magnificent five-star hotel and its structure is simply amazing. It has a lot of facilities with a beautiful gate, a huge terrace, and a big parking space. You can freely roam around everywhere. There are many rooms with unique windows. You love staying at this hotel. Initially, when you came in, you found it constricting, but as soon as you were given a room with all the wonderful amenities, you went in and first dropped down on the plush bed. You are enjoying your stay in the hotel.

However, one day you find that all of a sudden some smugglers have landed in the hotel. They have arrived in their helicopters. Some landed straight on the terrace and some in the spacious balcony. In a way, they have hijacked the hotel. They stay at the hotel for many days, troubling people, eating for free, and enjoying all the amenities. Adding insult to injury, while checking out, instead of paying the owner, they collect money from him!

This story is not of someone else; it's yours. The 5-star hotel is your body, created from the five elements of nature. You have received this body due to God's grace and you are the owner of this marvelous hotel. The smugglers that have barged in are negative emotions. Now, let's take a look to find out which parts of your body do these emotions barge in.

1. Close your eyes.
2. Observe each internal part of your body one by one. The different rooms in your hotel (body) are: the chest, above the navel, at the level of the navel, below the navel, on both sides of the navel, on the sides of the lungs, the back, etc. Check which emotion is residing in which room.
3. Each of these rooms have windows, which are the eyes, ears, nose, tongue, mouth, and skin, through which the emotions peek out. For example, when an emotion gets connected to the eyes, it expresses itself in the form of tears. There are emotions residing in many parts of your body. In this way, you are being held hostage by these emotions, and you need to achieve freedom from them.
4. Slowly open your eyes.

Through each of the five senses, the Self wishes to express itself in the highest way. The human body has been created for the supreme expression of the Self. This five-star hotel is a boon for you but turns into a curse when smugglers or negative emotions invade it. They invade you through the window of your heart and rob the wealth of your consciousness. Man is totally unaware of the harm caused by negative emotions. He is unable to stop the different emotions that emerge in his mind. Each of these emotions arrive in their own choppers and land either on the terrace (head) or in the balcony (heart) and enter your stomach, shoulders, back, or elsewhere. In this way, they break into different parts of your body.

Like, when someone's relative passes away suddenly, the emotion of fear first arrives in the heart and then passes through to the eyes. There are so many negative thoughts and emotions evoked by that event that tears start flowing from the eyes. When these emotions enter deep within, they cause grave problems such as a heart attack.

Each emotion chooses its own room, be it anger, fear, hatred, worry, or anxiety. Some people feel disgusted on seeing the face of a beggar, or watching someone picking their nose, or seeing garbage spilled around. This disgust occupies a specific room. When anxiety appears, it chooses its own room. Gradually, you will begin to know which emotion prefers which room, or which emotion occupies two rooms at a time. When you hear some bad news or feel frightened of something, then this emotion expands from one room to the other. Sometimes, it reaches your back and causes discomfort. How do you look at that emotion, and how should you actually watch it?

Feeding False Stories

When people stay in a five-star hotel, they pay for it. But, how much have your guests (emotions) paid you till date for staying in your hotel (body)? Think about this. Instead, they collect payment from you. When the emotion arrived, it was small and fragile. You gave it the chance to relax and be comfortable when you offered it a room.

Usually, when people enter a hotel room, they leave their luggage inside the door, and the first thing they do is flop down on the bed and stretch their body to rest and relax. Likewise, the emotion that arrives in your body is initially quite stiff and small, but then it spreads its legs and settles down. We commit the mistake of getting entangled with the emotion and offering it the best hospitality. We provide food of stories we have created to the emotions and fatten them up. Thereby, the emotion spreads and our body starts complaining of heaviness or burning. We feel this effect caused by the emotion on our body.

Since we continue to feed the emotion with false stories, it gets bigger and starts spreading around asking, "Where is my attached room?" For example, the attached room for the emotion of sorrow is the eyes. The emotion spreads to the eyes and tears start flowing. When sorrow first appears, it remains in its room. Tears don't flow at that time. When we begin to create stories in sorrow, that's when this emotion increases or intensifies. The stories could be: "Nobody likes me… nobody loves me or pays attention to me… everyone is biased against me… nobody listens to me…" By making up so many sad stories, we keep boosting our sorrow. That's how the sorrow swells and overflows as tears.

If the emotion of joy has appeared, and if it has spread throughout the room, then it too needs an attached room to spread further. Its attached room is the mouth. So, when the room within your body is unable to contain the joy, it spills out as laughter. The emotion of joy or happiness is not a smuggler; it's one of the good guys (positive emotions) and a dear friend. So, when each emotion fills up its room, it finds an attached room and comes out from there.

Let's learn in the next chapter what is the payment we should extract from the hotel guests or emotions.

FIVE-STAR HELL
Payment of Wisdom, Love, and Confidence

One, who is filled with negative emotions, lives each day of his life in a five-star hell. This is no ordinary hell. Man feels miserable over each emotion in this hell and wonders, "Why is this happening... why is that happening?" Negative emotions constantly arise within him, such as, "It's so boring... I am nervous... I am worried about my future... I'm furious... this is appalling... I hate him...."

If some terrorists (negative emotions) attack a hotel (body), they seize and capture the whole building. Their terror spreads throughout the structure. This is the reason why some people faint on encountering a fearful event. The horror shakes the foundation of the building and may even cause it to crumble down. People with a weak heart immediately suffer a heart attack.

The Practice of Wisdom

Until you receive wisdom and the understanding of how to practice it (*sadhana*), your hotel guests will not only pay you no money but instead will collect it from you. Suppose, an employee remains silent when his employer shouts at him or a daughter-in-law remains calm when her mother-in-law throws a tantrum. Who should be rewarded here: the one who is shouting or the one who remains calm? The reward should go to the one who maintains calm but in reality it happens the other way round.

You must first be convinced that you should collect payment from the guests that come to stay at your hotel. Next, to be able to collect the payment, you will have to practice being a detached witness. This is your *sadhana* or spiritual practice. You are the one seated in the main office, which is built in the center of the balcony (heart or the sacred space). You are the owner of this hotel. You, i.e. the real you, must gain knowledge and understanding of *sadhana* to be able to collect the payment.

The payment is wisdom, self-confidence, and love. Make sure that every emotion makes this payment before checking out. Your *sadhana* must begin as soon as an emotion arises—during the event, while walking, sitting, or whatever you are doing. Whenever you have the opportunity, close your eyes and watch your emotions intently. Whatever may be the duration of the emotion in your body, it must pay you with wisdom, self-confidence, and love. However, just the opposite happens. The emotion takes from you while leaving and you too pay it. In other words, the emotion harasses you, hurts you, and makes you miserable. You should have thought before paying, "Who should be paying? Why am I getting fooled?" Such mistakes need to stop.

To prevent such mistakes, you have to learn to watch each emotion with a sense of detachment. You must not serve it or feed it with stories, which makes it stronger and more dangerous. It is for you to decide whether to treat this emotion like a guest or as a paying guest. Had you fed the emotion the right food and prayed, it would have lost weight instead of gaining.

You must have the understanding that every emotion is your paying guest. It has arrived for some time and will soon leave. Before it leaves, it should pay you with self-confidence, awaken your wisdom, and teach you the importance of love. Only the right practice or *sadhana* will teach you the distinction between lust and love. If you are unable to collect the payment from emotions, you will always live in confusion.

People often make one more mistake. They get rid of one emotion, but instantly replace it with another. If there is lack of wisdom, then this other emotion causes even more suffering and you are unable to make any progress. Hence, it is important to learn the art of 'emptying' and being able to remain empty. Everyone should be aware of the art of staying empty in their free time and sowing the right seeds for the future. Otherwise, people get bored in their spare time and commit such mistakes that cause even more misery. It is therefore imperative to understand the practice (*sadhana*) of attaining freedom from emotions.

HOW TO COLLECT YOUR PAYMENT
Practice sadhana consistently

Our body has been created for the expression of love, bliss, and stillness (inner silence). However, as soon as any room in our hotel (body) is vacated by one emotion, it gets occupied by another. Additionally, we welcome each emotion with enthusiasm and feed it with our stories, making them stronger. After gaining the right understanding, we will not commit this error.

In our body, the nose is an attached room to several negative emotions. This means the breath changes with these emotions. This is an important point to be noted. If you want to know how far or deep an emotion has affected you, your breathing will be an indicator. Hence, you must focus on your breath. You can practice meditation on your breath. If you encounter anger, sorrow, or fear, at that time you must pay attention to your breath. The rate of breathing goes up or down depending on the intensity of your emotion. Whenever any such emotion overpowers you, you must work on your breath.

With every emotion, your breathing should be normal. When the body is filled with positive thoughts, then positive emotions reside within the rooms. However, once they leave, the negative emotions immediately barge into the rooms. This is detrimental for your body. When there is no emotion spreading to the nose, then the nose is only functioning to take in oxygen. When a negative emotion appears, your rate of breathing decreases, which reduces the supply of oxygen to your body. This is very harmful. Therefore, always ensure that while facing a negative news, your breathing remains normal. Listen to the news with detachment. If your breathing slows, you instantly give the emotion a chance to get inside you.

Despite the negative emotion, if you consciously maintain normal breathing, you will find that the emotion is gradually losing its strength. In our daily lives, a lot of minor negative events keep occurring. If you pay attention to your breath during those events, the triggered emotions will lose their power. You will then say, "Though the negative emotion arrived and stayed for some time, it paid me the rent—the rent of self-confidence."

To stop your paying guests from dominating you, it is important to enhance your wisdom. You must achieve such a state that as soon as a paying guest arrives, it should pay you and leave at once. This means, any positive or negative emotion should pay you in the form of love, faith, bliss, wisdom, or stillness. If your awareness and understanding is rising with the arrival of paying guests, it indicates you are moving in the right direction.

You must watch all emotions not holding your breath but with a smile. Your hotel (body) is amazing and good paying guests should always come to stay in it.

If you feel despondent with any emotion, it means that emotion has collected payment from you. That's not all, it has left its kids with you as well. These kids are the thoughts of your negative past events. These kids are now growing within you because you are nourishing them with your tales. In this way, the suppressed emotions of past events form emotional knots in your mind. We remain completely unaware of how these knots got created.

If you practice your *sadhana* regularly with the right understanding, these kids will all start coming out from within you. You will slowly begin to empty. It is important to stay alert after getting empty, as you do not want negative thoughts to again arrive and reside within you. When you are filled with love, bliss, and silence, your body will give you joy your entire lifetime.

If you have become an expert at collecting payment, then even if a mammoth negative emotion arrives like a terrorist, you won't fear it. That's because you have become so proficient in your *sadhana* that you can very smartly collect payment from that terrorist.

You paint and prepare your hotel (body) in such a way that no weather change (joy or sorrow, pleasant or unpleasant emotions) can damage your body, and no storm can shake its foundation. If you have this self-confidence, that's your payment. Each day, ask yourself, "Am I getting my payment or not?" From now on, you will collect your amount from every emotion and tell it, "You are a paying guest in this body and you have to pay me. I let you stay here, so you must pay now and leave." In this way, every minor or major, genuine or pseudo emotion, will vacate your body.

Pseudo emotions are those that arise when nothing has actually happened. But due to an illusion, an emotion arises. For instance, you screamed when you believed a rope to be a snake in the dark. This is an example of pseudo emotion. Because of your shrieks, the lights of the entire hotel (body) came on, only to find that it was just a piece of rope! There was no cause for the terrifying emotion; your mind made up a story that it's a deadly snake, which triggered the emotion of fear. If you don't feed emotions with your tales, you will come to know how fake those emotions are. You felt as if a guest had arrived, when actually it had not.

Practice for liberation from emotions—*sadhana*

With the practice of *sadhana*, all work is accomplished in the best possible manner. But one commits mistakes due to ignorance about practicing sadhana the right way. Every situation in life is signaling to discard the old labels and look at things with a new perspective. However big an emotion, practice watching it with happiness.

People often ask, "When I get angry, what should I do?" They are advised, "Whatever you do or say during anger, is always going to be wrong. The best option is to stay silent when angry. But for this, regular practice of your sadhana is important." Whether or not you encounter a negative event or thought, you must commit to practicing your sadhana every day. Both negative and positive events keep occurring in the present time, although you feel wretched by remembering the events of the past too. All these emotions should be taken as an opportunity to practice sadhana. On the other hand, if they make you feel even more dismal, it means they conned you into paying them.

You deserve to be rewarded if you kept your calm despite your boss yelling at you. The reward is self-confidence. If you are developing the self-confidence that you can face any emotion without being consumed by it, that's a sign of progressing in the right direction. Otherwise, man is losing his self-confidence day by day. "My boss is horrible... I hate my job..." and so on. If you switch to another company with such thoughts, you will again find yourself in a similar situation.

You should reflect on why difficult and dissatisfying things come into your life. The reason is that you attracted the new job from the platform of misery. You will attract the wrong people everywhere if your belief is "people are wrong." That is why, you must harbor the right understanding.

Guests of Equanimity, Understanding, and Awareness

Once again remember that if you suffer and feel upset due to any emotion, that means *you* are paying it. Instead you have to collect the payment of love, joy, and stillness from them. It would become so simple for you if the guest of happiness arrives at your hotel. You would want to live your whole life with happiness.

If your happiness is maintained be it joy or sorrow, if you are able to stay happy every moment, then suddenly one day you will realize that you have reached Supreme Consciousness (seventh level of Consciousness). Thereafter, everything can be accomplished with bliss. To make this possible, you must always keep the guests of Equanimity, Understanding, and Awareness in your hotel. If these guests are with you all the time, then you will always have a smile on your face.

Your smile won't slip even when sometimes the guests of problems or stress come visiting. You will be able to declare: "Whoever the guest may be, my menu is ready. I will no longer get caught in their web. Till today I was suffering because I was getting trapped by them and they were depleting my accounts [lowering my level of consciousness]. I was unable to decipher the reason for this, but now I understand everything."

If the approaching guests are given the right signal, the smugglers of thoughts will stop coming. Due to ignorance and unconsciousness, one sends the wrong signals, which allow the negative emotions into the hotel. For example, if you put up a sign of 'Boredom' at your hotel balcony, then all emotions related to it will arrive. Man tends to do many wrong things in boredom. He places the wrong signboards on his own hotel (body), which allows the negative emotions in. Now the time has come to become aware and get free from such emotions. If you are aware, negative emotions will stop arriving. And even if occasionally the emotion of sorrow or fear arrives, you will collect payment from it and get rid of it right away.

When people hear thunder and lightning, they often make up a story by thinking that perhaps the lightning is going to strike their home. If there is a power failure, people curse the electricity board. But now you must watch every emotion without fear or blame. Your understanding would be, "If there is a power failure, it means that's what is needed at this moment." You will accept the situation and continue practicing your sadhana.

Then you will find that with sadhana, your self-confidence, love, and wisdom is growing every day. Your conviction of "I am not the body" is also rising. You are separate from the body and you watch with the eyes of wisdom that the guest which has arrived is transient, and with time it keeps changing. When you observe the guest as a detached witness, you will never cause any harm to yourself. This is the art that needs to be imbibed. This is what will help you attain emotional freedom.

When you have mastered this art and achieved emotional maturity, you will then be ready to attain spiritual maturity. This will in turn help you to fulfil the ultimate purpose of your life, which is getting established in your true divine self and expressing its divine qualities.

* * *

You can send your opinion or feedback on this book to :

Tejgyan Foundation, Pimpri Colony, P. O. Box 25,
Pimpri, Pune – 411017 (Maharashtra), INDIA
email : mail@tejgyan.com

APPENDIX

APPENDIX

About Sirshree

Sirshree's spiritual quest, which began during his childhood, led him on a journey through various schools of thought and prevalent meditation practices. His overpowering desire to attain the Truth made him relinquish his teaching profession. After a long period of contemplation on the truth of life, his spiritual quest culminated in the attainment of the ultimate truth. Since then, over the last two decades, he has dedicated his life toward elevating mass consciousness and making spiritual pursuit simple and accessible to all.

Sirshree espouses, "**All paths that lead to the truth begin differently, but culminate at the same point – understanding. Understanding is complete in itself. Listening to this understanding is enough to attain the truth.**"

Sirshree has delivered more than 3000 discourses that throw light on this understanding, simplify various aspects of life and unravel missing links in spirituality. He delivers the understanding in casual contemporary language by weaving profound aspects into analogies, parables and humor that provoke one to contemplate.

To make it possible for people from all walks of life to directly experience this understanding, Sirshree has designed the *Maha Aasmani Param Gyan Shivir* – a retreat designed as a comprehensive system for imparting wisdom. This system for wisdom, which has been accredited with ISO 9001:2015 certification, has inspired thousands of seekers from all walks of life to progress on their journey of the Truth. This system makes the wisdom accessible to every human being, regardless of religion, caste, social strata, country or belief system.

Sirshree is the founder of Tej Gyan Foundation, a no-profit organization committed to raising mass consciousness with branches in India, the United States, Europe and Asia-Pacific. Sirshree's retreats have transformed the lives of thousands and his teachings have inspired various social initiatives for raising global consciousness.

His published work includes more than 100 books, some of which have been translated in more than 10 languages and published by leading publishers. Sirshree's books provide profound and practical reading on existential subjects like emotional maturity, harmony in relationships, developing self-belief, overcoming stress and anxiety, and dealing with the question of life-beyond-death, to name a few. His literature on core spirituality expounds the deeper meaning of self-realization and self-stabilization, unravelling missing links in the understanding of karma, wisdom, devotion, meditation and consciousness.

Various luminaries and celebrities like His Holiness the Dalai Lama, publishers Mr. Reid Tracy, Ms. Tami Simon and Yoga Master Dr. B. K. S. Iyengar have released Sirshree's books and lauded his work. "The Source" book series, authored by Sirshree, has sold over 10 million copies in 5 years. His book, "The Warrior's Mirror", published by Penguin, was featured in the Limca Book of Records for being released on the same day in 11 languages.

Tejgyan... The Road Ahead
What is Tejgyan?

Tejgyan is the wisdom of the existential truth, which is beyond duality. "Gyan" is a term commonly used for "knowledge". Tejgyan is the wisdom beyond knowledge and ignorance. It is understanding that arises from direct experience of the final truth. It is what sets us free from the limitations of the mind and opens us to our highest potential.

In today's world, there are people who feel disharmony and are desperately trying to achieve balance in an unpredictable life. Tejgyan helps them in harmonizing with their true nature, the Self, thereby restoring balance in all aspects of their lives.

And then, there are those who are successful, but feel a sense of emptiness within. Tejgyan provides them fulfilment and helps them to embark on a journey towards self-realization. There are others who feel lost and are seeking the meaning of life. Tejgyan helps them to realize the true purpose of human life.

All this is possible with Tejgyan due to a very simple reason. The experience of the ultimate truth (God or Pure consciousness) is always available. The direct experience of this truth is possible provided the right method is known. Tejgyan is that method, that understanding.

The understanding of Tejgyan makes it possible to lead a life of freedom from fear, worry, anger and stress. It helps in attaining physical vitality, emotional strength and stability, harmony in relationships, financial freedom and spiritual progress.

At Tej Gyan Foundation, Sirshree imparts this understanding through a System for Wisdom – a series of retreats that guides participants step by step towards realizing the true Self, being established in the experience of self-realization, and expressing its qualities. This system for wisdom has been accredited with the ISO 9001:2015 certification.

Maha Aasmani Param Gyan Shivir

"**Maha Aasmani Param Gyan Shivir**" is the flagship Self-realization retreat offered by Tej Gyan Foundation. The retreat is conducted in Hindi. The teachings of the retreat are non-denominational (secular).

This residential retreat is held for 3 to 5 days at the foundation's MaNaN Ashram amidst the glory of the mountains and the pristine beauty of nature. The Ashram is located at the outskirts of the city of Pune in India, and is well connected by air, road and rail. The retreat is also held at other centres of Tej Gyan Foundation across the world.

You can participate in this retreat to attain ageless wisdom through a unique System for Wisdom so that you can:

1. Discover "Who am I" through direct experience.
2. Learn to abide in pure consciousness while functioning in the world, allowing the qualities of consciousness like peace, love, joy, compassion, abundance and creativity to manifest.
3. Acquire simple tools to use in everyday life, which help quiet the chattering mind.
4. Get practical techniques to be in the present and connect to the source of all answers within (the inner guru).

5. Discover missing links in the practices of Meditation (*Dhyana*), Action (*Karma*), Wisdom (*Gyana*) and Devotion (*Bhakti*).
6. Understand the nature of your body-mind mechanism to attain freedom form its tendencies.
7. Learn practical methods to shift from mind-centered living to consciousness-centered living.

A Mini-retreat is also conducted, especially for teenagers (14 to 16 years of age) during summer and winter vacations.

To register for retreats, visit www.tejgyan.org, contact (+91) 9921008060, or email mail@tejgyan.com

About Tej Gyan Foundation

Tej Gyan Foundation (TGF) was established with the mission of creating a highly evolved society through all-round development of every individual that transforms all the facets of their lives. It is a non-profit organization, founded on the teachings of Sirshree.

The Foundation has received the ISO certification (ISO 9001:2015) for its system of imparting wisdom. It has centres all across India as well as in other countries. The motto of Tej Gyan Foundation is 'Happy Thoughts'.

At the core of the philosophy of Tejgyan is the Power of Acceptance. Acceptance has profound meaning and is at the core of our Being. It is Acceptance that brings forth true love, joy and peace.

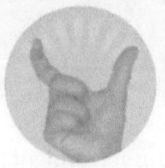

Symbol of Acceptance

The Symbol of Acceptance – shown above – is a representation of this truth. The symbol represents brackets. Whatever occurs in life falls within these brackets that signify acceptance of whatever is. Hence, this symbol forms the centerpiece of the Foundation's MaNaN Ashram.

The Foundation is creating a highly evolved society through:

- Tejgyan Programs (Retreats, YouTube Webcasts)
- Tejgyan Books and Apps
- Tejgyan Projects (Value education, Women empowerment, Peace initiatives)

The Foundation undertakes projects to elevate the level of consciousness among students, youth, women, senior citizens, teachers, doctors, leaders, professionals, corporate and Government organizations, police force, prisoners etc.

Now you can register online for the following retreats

Maha Aasmani Param Gyan Shivir
(5 Days Residential Retreat in Hindi)

Mini Maha Aasmani Shivir
3 Days (Residential) Retreat for Teens

www.tejgyan.org

Books can be delivered at your doorstep by registered post or courier. You can request the same through postal money order or pay by VPP. Please send the money order to either of the following two addresses:

WOW Publishings Pvt. Ltd.

1. Registered Office: E-4, Vaibhav Nagar, Near Tapovan Mandir, Pimpri, Pune - 411017.

2. Post Box No. 36, Pimpri Colony Post Office, Pimpri, Pune - 411017

Phone No: (+91) 9011013210 / 9623457873

You can also order your copy at the online store:
www.gethappythoughts.org
*Free Shipping plus 10% Discount on purchases above Rs. 500/-

For further details contact:
Tejgyan Global Foundation
Registered Office:
Happy Thoughts Building, Vikrant Complex, Near Tapovan Mandir, Pimpri, Pune 411017, Maharashtra, India.
Contact No: 020-27411240, 27412576
Email: mail@tejgyan.com

MaNaN Ashram:
Survey No. 43, Sanas Nagar, Nandoshi gaon, Kirkatwadi Phata, Sinhagad Road, Tal. Haveli, Dist. Pune 411024, Maharashtra, India.
Contact No: 992100 8060.
Hyderabad: 9885558100, **Bangalore:** 9880412588,
Delhi : 9891059875, **Nashik:** 9326967980, **Mumbai:** 9373440985

For accessing our unique 'System for Wisdom' from self-help to self-realization, please follow us on:

	Website Online Shopping/ Blog	www.tejgyan.org www.gethappythoughts.org
	Video Channel	www.youtube.com/tejgyan For Q&A videos: http://goo.gl/YA81DQ
	Social networking	www.facebook.com/tejgyan
	Social networking	www.twitter.com/sirshree
	Internet Radio	http://www.tejgyan.org/ internetradio.aspx

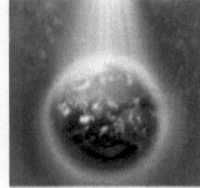

Pray for World Peace along with thousands of others every day at 09:09am and 09:09pm

Divine Light of Love, Bliss and Peace is Showering;
The Golden Light of Higher Consciousness is Rising;
All negativity on Earth is Dissolving;
Everyone is in Peace and Blissfully Shining;
O God, Gratitude for Everything!

www.ingramcontent.com/pod-product-compliance
Lightning Source LLC
LaVergne TN
LVHW040148080526
838202LV00042B/3075